1

The Sum of My Mistakes

3/25/12

TO:
Cee Cee
Thanks for your support!

Love

5

The Sum of My Mistakes

By

Dawn L. Fortè

Published by
Amorous Ink Publishing
3416 N. Shadeland Ave.
Indianapolis, IN 46226

ISBN 978-0-9849630-4-1

Printed in the United States of America

Dedication & Thank You !

I'd like to dedicate this book to My four Wonderful Children... Brandon H. Forte', Kameera T McQuitter-Forte', Nivek T. Forte' and Tyray R. Forte', and to my two beautiful grand children Anyea K Forte' and Zakhi A. Johnson. Also to David T. Holmes at It's A Wrap Cafe. If it wasn't for them this book wouldn't have ever happened. I LOVE YOU So MUCH!

Thank you / Acknowledgements

First and foremost I have to thank my Lord and Savior Jesus Christ! Without all of his blessings I never would have been able to write this book.

I'd like to thank my kids for believing in me and being so supportive and just always having my back. Brandon, Kameera, Nivek and Tyray I adore you guys!!

I'd like to thank my family, my wonderful daddy Henry E. Forte for believing in me and my beautiful mommy Evelyn L. Forte. My sisters Kim McNair, Robin Nwabara and Roni Allen and Clem Mensah. My brother Riki Forte and sister-in-law Movicia Mozingo-Forte for all of their support.

To my biggest supporters in addition to my family, David T. Holmes and Natwan Jenkins Owner and Managering Partner at It's A Wrap Cafe in Plainfield, NJ for putting up with me for so many months along with the rest of my It's A Wrap Family, thank you ladies for being so sweet. No one has ever treated me so good and with so much love and encouragement, I love you guys so much!

Next, I have to thank Lisa Robinson-Burgess and Tanesha Pannell for reading all of my ideas and giving me their honest opinions, and Candice Brown for all of her help also. You ladies are so sweet!

To Kat Carnegie my PIC (Partner In Crime) for our long walks and talks. You were really there for me Kat and I love you and Rick so much.

To everyone who stopped by the cafe while I was writing Kim, LaToya,

Tiwana, James and everyone else, to give me some love, encouragement and support I did not forget you. I may not have named you all, but I have a lot of love in my heart for you. To my FB family...You guys are the best!

A special thank you also to Anthony H. Bell for introducing me to my Publisher... a thousand thank you's!

To my Publisher and Editor Dawn Blanchard (Deep Rivers) and Gerald Johnson Jr. (Damien Darke) thank you so much for everything. You guys have taught me so much. And

FINALLY... to you who purchased my first novel thank you a million times for your support!

-Dawn :-)

The Sum of My Mistakes
A Novel by Dawn L. Forte'

"You are fifty fucking years old! FIFTY... and you are doing the same shit in this very different day! What in the hell is wrong with you? And why would you drag me into your bullshit? I hate you! I fucking HATE you! NO... I'm not saying it because I'm mad, I actually hate you, every inch of you, especially that little ass dick of yours. Yeah I said it, your little ass dick! Now fuck with me!" Evan Roberts just smiled and gathered his things to leave. He could care less what Saniya said about his dick. He had been ramming that dick inside of her for the past six months with no complaints from her until today, when once again he got caught with his dick in a place where it shouldn't have been. In the mouth of his newest sales person Mrs. Macy Long.

Being the CEO of Chef Life enterprises, a culinary supply company, he could care less what anyone thought of him. He was the shit as far has he was concerned.

Evan was actually quite tickled at the fit Saniya was having. To him

that meant that she cared. Saniya refused to stop him from leaving this

time. This time she wanted him to go. This time once again, she was done

with Evan Roberts.

Evan stopped in front of the large mahogany dresser with the mirror on

top and glanced at himself. He was starting to look his age. His flawless

almond colored skin looked a little dry and was beginning to sag a little.

Tiny lines were forming around his mouth and his eyes. His beautiful light

brown eyes looked blood shot and tired. His goatee seemed to have a few

more gray hairs in it than he remembers he saw this morning. All that

running around eventually takes a toll on you, he thought to himself. I

can't let any of these women catch me out there. I don't know if I ever

want to be tied down like that again. I guess I should have let Saniya know

that from the start of things huh? Whatever. She'll get over it. She always

takes me back. ALWAYS. This little "break up" won't do anything but

allow me the time to finish off the blow job Macy Long started on me but

was rudely interrupted by Saniya barging into my office unannounced.

She claimed she wanted to surprise me with lunch, but she just wanted to

catch me out there and if you seek you shall find. She sought and she found. I guess I shouldn't have smiled when she called my dick little. I know plenty of women in the last few months that wouldn't agree with Saniya's opinion of my dick. She damn sure wasn't complaining when she was choking on it last night. What a difference a day makes. I can't believe she's still yelling and screaming at me.

"And you know what else Evan, you're immature and selfish!" Yadda yadda yadda I'm thinking to myself. I'm not selfish bitch I'm Evan Roberts... I'm big shit why don't you get that? Sometimes woman say stupid shit out of their mouths when they get upset. "Saniya, why didn't you tell me all of this shit within the last six months? If I had known you felt this way about me, I would have dumped your ass months ago." I yelled at her. Yeah, I know I shouldn't have said it, but she is blowing this shit WAY out of proportion.

Saniya had finally had enough. She was so sick and tired of being sick and tired again. "Evan, get the fuck out!" She yelled at me. See, this is where I get angry.

"Bitch, don't you ever tell me to get out of anywhere I'm paying for! This isn't your house Saniya! I pay the bills around here! I will leave when I fucking feel like it and not before! I'm the millionaire here! I'm the one with the money and the power in this relationship and I will do what the hell I want when I want! Now sit the hell down and shut the hell up for a change. I'm tired of your damn voice!"

The Sum of My Mistakes
Chapter Two

Saniya

"No this negro did not just call me a bitch! Did he just tell me to shut up?

Did he just tell me he's not going anywhere? I'm going to lose my mind!

I'm going to lose my f'n mind! I'm trying to keep cool but this man brings

out the worst in me. Six months of this bullshit. Six months of my life

wasted. Evan makes you want to kill his ass. All of these crazy thoughts

running through my head right now. If I kill this man will the Lord and his

family forgive me? I'm very serious right now. I want to take a knife and

cut his heart out, if he even has one. I can't believe I caught him

again. Three times in six months."

I wasn't shocked when I walked in and found his dick in that slut

Macy's mouth. Evan has a very healthy sexual appetite. I'm beginning to

think he's a sex addict. It's so funny every time something seems excessive

to us we want to say it's an addiction. Although I believe that there are sex addicts that exist, I think I'm just trying to find an excuse for Evan's behavior. In my mind if I affiliate his behavior with a disease or disorder, maybe I can help him and things will get better between us. I'm just fooling myself. Evan is just a selfish asshole with a lot of money and some good dick but that's it. He's arrogant and cut throat. No wonder his marriage fell apart, he's horrible. One thing about this entire situation he's right, I have no control over what he does and when he comes and goes from this house. He owns it and pays all of the bills. It wasn't exactly my idea for me to give up my apartment, quit my job and stay home and take care of this house, Evan talked a good talk and I just knew he would take care of me for the rest of my life. I just didn't realize the price I would have to pay for finally finding a man to take care of me, especially with a past like mine. I have not been the most stand-up legitimate citizen. I used to be in the street pharmaceutical business and I'm a former dancer and porn star. People think that thick girls can't become dancers or porn stars. Don't be fooled. I was in the business for many years and I made a hell of a lot of money.

My dancer name was Sweet Serenity which was also my porn name. I've done a couple hundred movies and danced in a few clubs in the tri-state area. I got that name from an ex who said my pussy is the sweetest he's ever tasted.

I loved my dancing job. I loved the attention and the money. I didn't feel like a big girl when I danced, I just felt like the most beautiful woman in the world. Men wanted to touch me but couldn't. I loved watching them throw money at me and telling me I'm sexy. All of that attention and all of that money, it was great. I guess I have a few self-esteem issues. With my past and obviously now my present relationship going to hell, I guess I don't think my self-esteem is very high. I know this and you would think that because I know what the problem is I could work on fixing it, but I just don't know how.

When I met Evan 1 year ago, I thought he could help all of my problems go away. He was so sweet in the beginning. So patient with me and so kind. Why do men do that? Chase you down and pursue you, and when they finally get you, treat you like shit?

I met Evan at the gym I used to go to. He is a good friend of my former personal trainer Sebastian. Mmm, talk about sexy. Sebastian is fine as hell with a beautiful body and the personality to match. Anyway, I was working out when Evan came in to train with Sebastian. My training session had gone over its regular time and I was getting ready to leave. Evan walked in looking so fine. I tried like hell not to pay him any attention. Sebastian must have felt our connection so he introduced Evan and me. I gave a quick hello and then got the hell out of that gym. I've never had such an instant connection with anyone not even my daughter Azera's father. Well he must have felt it too because he started showing up early to all of his sessions with Sebastian. He always had a beautiful smile and bottle of grape Propel fitness water for me. I guess he noticed what I was drinking from the first time we met. Sebastian told me he had been asking about me ever since the day we met. He pursued me relentlessly for six months always asking me out to lunch or for coffee, but I would always say I was busy or I had to get home to my daughter. Finally Sebastian said he thought Evan was a good catch and that I should stop acting so stuck up and go out with him. So I took Sebastian's advice and agreed to a date with Evan. Our first date was wonderful. It was

January 7Th. I remember because I journal everything. Evan came to pick me up at 8:00pm. We went to this lovely restaurant called Aariangs on Rt. 22 in Mountainside NJ. It's a Hibachi and Sushi restaurant where they prepare the food right in front of you. We had so much fun on our first night out. It wasn't a stuck up or stuffy date. We left Aariang's as it was closing. We were having so much fun we lost all track of time.

Evan opened doors for me; He pulled out my chair for me to sit down. He helped me order my food and was very friendly with the couple sitting next to us. I was extremely impressed with him. I just don't know what happened from then to now. He's so different, so not the same man he was 6 months ago.

I'm scared to leave the house now. I fear this dam fool will have the locks changed before I get a chance to come back and get my things. Seriously, where in the hell am I going to go? Nobody knows what's going on with me and Evan. I couldn't tell my family how he's been behaving because there are so many haters in my family who got an attitude with me when I started seeing Evan. I don't have the heart to face them and to tell them what I've been going through the past three months of our relationship.

With my past, my family won't give a shit what happens to me if I mess this up. Funny, how they would think I'm messing this up no matter how much I explain to them that I've been the perfect girlfriend. At least I've tried to be.

Now what do I do? I feel stupid sitting here quiet and fuming all at the same time. I'm glad my daughter isn't home right now. I wouldn't want her to see her mother being shut down by this dam fool. Mark my words Evan will regret the day he disrespected me and called me out of my name and the times he cheated on me and slept with other women. Oh yes, payback is a bitch.

The Sum of My Mistakes

Chapter Three

Evan

Ha... got her! She's not going to talk shit to me in my own damn house.
Fuck that I pay the bills in this house. So what I was getting my dick
sucked. Why do women get so damn emotional over such trivial shit? I
don't want that damn girl. I just wanted her to pleasure me. It's all about
me, when is Saniya going to realize that? When is she going to learn to
play by my rules? Now her ass knows. I didn't want to call her a bitch but
I knew that would get her attention. It definitely shut her ass up. I'm not
going to have some ex dancer/porn star telling me what the hell is going to
happen with my life! She will shut the hell up and take whatever I give
her. Macy gives good ass head. If Saniya had any sense she would thank
her for making me feel good for those few minutes. Shit I was coming

home to her tonight. I get very angry when I have to go through unnecessary stress.

I need a drink and a shower. All this tension in the air, I'm going out and have myself a drink. Give Macy a call and see if she can meet me. Saniya needs some time to herself to think about what happened here tonight. This should teach her a serious lesson about fucking with me. She wanted me, this is what she gets. Ring...Ring... Ring...Ring... "Hello."

"Macy, Hey what's up, it's Evan. How are you?"

"I'm good Evan, how are you?"

"I'm good, a little stressed out. Sorry about what happened today. Sometimes my lady can get, shall we say a little insecure."

"Oh I can understand that, it was a bit embarrassing in the position I was in."

"Yes I know, so what are you doing tonight?" I asked Macy.

"Nothing, just relaxing why what's up?" she asked me sounding anxious. That's what I like about Macy she always got right to the point. She knows what I like. I could never have her as my girl but she's good for a blow job or two. "I'm going out for a drink, I would love for you to join me, and can you get away?" I asked getting right to the point myself.

"Sure, give me like 20 minutes Evan. Where would you like for me to meet you?"

"Do you know where Studio 44 is on Watchung Ave. in Plainfield?"

"Yes I do" She replied.

"OK, I will be there in about 30 minutes."

"OK, I'll see you then."

"Cool." Click. I hung up. Yes! I need to relieve some tension. Macy has the perfect skills for what I need tonight. She's freaky as hell and likes making me feel good. I knew the day I hired her that she would be one of my "special" employees. Having this much power should be a sin. I'm rich, I'm good looking, I have a fine as woman and all the pussy I can ask for, when I want it and how I want it. Saniya will just have to go with the flow. As long as I'm not bringing any women to the house and fucking them literally in front of her, she has nothing to say as far as I'm concerned.

I went upstairs, got in the shower and changed my clothes. I wanted to make sure I was ready to handle my business when I met up with Macy. I knew Saniya wouldn't be happy with me leaving but she's just going to have to deal with it. After I was done getting dressed I went downstairs and grabbed my keys. Then I headed to the door. I stopped to say goodbye to Saniya.

"Saniya, I'm going to have a drink and to get some air. I'll be home soon. No response. "Is Azera coming home tonight?"

"Yes" was all she would say to me.

"OK well see you later, I love you Saniya" I said to see if that would soften her up.

"Bye Evan." Hmm one and two word answers, no I love you too. She's really pissed off this time. That's ok, she'll live. She always does. Saniya isn't going anywhere. She's in love with me and I'm in love with her, I'm just doing me right now. Maybe one day I'll marry her and do right by her, but for now, I'm having some fun. When and if I'm ready I'll make her my wife and we'll live happily ever after, right now I'm going to meet Macy and see how much she really likes me.

The Sum of My Mistakes

Chapter Four

Macy

Mr. Evan Roberts. Oh yeah! I can't wait to see him. After we were so rudely interrupted by that bitch girlfriend of his, I thought I'd never see him again. At the very least I thought she would make him fire me. I guess now I know who has the control in that so-called relationship. I know one day I'll have Mr. Roberts all to myself; right now I have to play the jump off role. That's cool because when I'm done he won't be able to breathe without me.

I don't want to dress too fly. I still need for him to think I'm the poor little young girl that doesn't know any better. I hope he lets me taste him again. Having his dick in my mouth made me feel good, it made me feel sexy.

Sex can make a woman feel very powerful. Being able to give good head is a really sensual expression of how you feel about someone. Men love good head. I've heard it described as an extremely euphoric experience. I guess what it's like when you have a man who knows how to eat good pussy. Some men say I'm just freaky as hell. I guess they just can't hang. I'm no holds barred. I like it any way and any place I can get it. I love sex... and I love men. I have had a woman a time or two, but I love the feel of a man, the way they smell and how hard and forceful they are when they get horny. I guess I am a little freaky. We'll see how freaky Mr. Roberts lets me get with him tonight.

I guess I'll wear my little black dress with no panties. Take a few condoms just in case things don't work out with him and I meet someone else tonight. For a young girl I have a lot of experience.

Finally I'm dressed. It felt like it took me forever. Let me head out, I'm so late. I'm always late, dam I hope he didn't leave. I headed down Rt. 22 West and got off on the Somerset St. exit. I made a left off of the ramp and another quick left onto Codington Ave by the KFC. I made a right at the next corner and headed down Watchung Ave. I went down a few blocks and finally made it to the club. Here we are at Studio 44. I immediately saw that black Mercedes in the parking lot with the custom license plates. "Chef 365 "Oh good, he's here!" Ok that's way too much excitement I thought to myself. Let me keep my cool.

Let me give him a call and let him know I'm here. Ring...Ring... "Hello"
"Hi Mr. Roberts, it's me Macy."
"Hello Macy, I guess you're not going to be able to make it tonight?"
"No I'm here; I'm getting out of my car now and getting ready to walk in."
"Oh ok, I'm at the last seat at the bar."
"Ok, be right there." I said trying not to sound like a giddy school girl.
"Sounds good." Evan replied...
Click...we both hung up
"Ok now it's show time".

I walked into the bar and it was really nice. Perfect place to relax and have a drink. I spotted Evan in the very last seat at the bar looking very handsome. He went from his very expensive Armani suit earlier today to a complete Navy blue Polo sweat suit with a white Polo tee shirt and a matching blue Polo pullover. His outfit was complete with navy blue

Polo tennis shoes. He was clean shaven with a fresh new haircut. I know it was all for me. Evan is very sexy. All 6'4" 235 pounds of him.

I wanted him to do me right on the bar in front of everyone, but I had to keep it cool. I had to keep my nerves calm and be mature about this situation. My pussy began to get warm and throb at the sight of him. At that moment I wish I had worn underwear just in case I began to get really wet. My breasts, a perfect 32C cup, got very hard and began to tingle. My entire body got hot. I wanted him so bad I could taste him. I was so wrapped up in how Evan looked that

I didn't even notice the bitch leaning on the bar flirting with him. It startled me and made me re-think my approach. How dare he, I thought to myself. Didn't I tell him that I was on my way in? How dare he be talking to someone else while I'm walking in? OK, calm down girl and play this cool. I decided to walk over to where them and get rid of that trick a look. I pushed my titties up high and stuck my ass out. I sashayed over to where they were and shot that bitch a look. She didn't even budge. Just totally disrespected me and kept talking to Evan. "Hey you", I said to Evan like the chick wasn't even there.

"Hi Macy, how are you?" he said without even a glimpse of a smile. The bitch stood up straight, looked me up and down and then told Evan she would give him a call tomorrow. Never taking her eyes off of me. That's right bitch look! I thought to myself. I wanted to pull the ugly lace-front wig she was wearing right off of her head. Instead, I flashed a big smile on my face and slid into the bar stool right next to Evan. "Nice place" I said to ease some of the tension that I felt coming from Evan.

"Yeah, I like it, good food, good drinks, and a nice atmosphere" he said without even looking at me. He seemed to be totally in another world. "Would you like a drink Macy?" he asked me finally looking at me. "Yes, I'll take a Malibu bay breeze please." He got up from the bar stool and walked down to the other end of the bar to get my drink. As he stood up I noticed he was rock hard and the front of his pants was really sticking out. He noticed me smiling at his manhood and he smiled back at me. Now, that's more like it.

I sat on the bar stool with my back turned to the rest of the bar area. It was taking Evan a long ass time to get my drink. I didn't want to appear to be looking for him so I dare not turn around. Instead I reached into my purse and retrieved my foundation compact with the mirror and opened it up. I acted like I was retouching my makeup and positioned the mirror to see what was going on behind me. There was Evan, leaning over talking to the female bartender. He was smiling at her, but he could hardly look at me the entire time I've been here. Hump! He actually kissed her on the cheek! Oh no he didn't! I thought to myself. Keep cool Macy, don't blow this. They are just conversations; he's not fucking anyone else, just you I told myself. I saw Evan stand up and then pick up the two drinks the bartender placed on the bar. He turned and started walking towards me. Finally! I mumbled to myself. I closed my compact and placed it back into my purse. I straightened out my facial expression just as Evan made it back to our end of the bar. Evan handed me my drink and then sat back down next to me. He wasn't one for too much conversation tonight. He seemed totally uninterested in me. I guess he has a few things on his mind.

"Are you ok Mr. Roberts?" I asked him to break up some of the tension.

"Yeah Macy, I'm fine, why did you ask me that?"

"Because you don't seem like yourself."

"Macy, you don't even know who I am, how do you know whether I'm acting like myself or not?" Wow, that was kind of harsh.

"I'm sorry, I was just asking." I said with a pitiful look on my face.

"No I'm sorry Macy, I guess I have a few things on my mind and I snapped at you, I apologize."

"It's ok, I can go and let you handle whatever it is you feel you need to handle." I said, while acting like I was gathering my things to leave. Then his words stunned me. "No I'd rather take you outside to my car and watch you finish sucking my dick like we were doing earlier." Wow...this guy is bold as hell! I had to come up with a good reply.

"I have an even better idea, I whispered to him. "Why don't we go back to your office and finish where we left off."

"Dam, that sure sounds good to me." Evan finally said with a big smile on his face. We walked out of the club and got into our separate cars. Evan's office is about a 30 minute drive to Newark. He pulled his car out in front of mine and headed towards Rt. 22 east bound to Newark. I followed close by headed in the same direction. He drove very fast the few minutes it took to get to Newark. We got off of Rt.22 and headed to McCarter Highway to Broad St. where the office building was located. We reached D Love LLC. and pulled all the way into the very back lot where it was nice and dark and secluded. Evan got out of his car first and started walking straight into the back of the building. I got out of my car and ran a little to catch up to him and followed close behind him. I thought he was headed up to his office but he instead he took me to an empty office in the back of the building. Once in there, he closed the door behind us and immediately sat in the empty chair behind the large wooden desk. He pulled his pants completely off, folded them and placed them on another empty chair in the room. He grabbed his dick which wasn't fully hard yet. He never said a word, just sat there with his dick in his right hand. He stroked himself a few times, and then pointed his index finger and curled it back to gesture me to come to him. He watched me slowly walk closer to him. I stopped right in front of the chair mere inches away from his big black juicy dick. My entire body got horny again. I could have sworn my lips began to tingle and my mouth watered. I leaned forward to give him a kiss on his lips, but he grabbed my head and pushed it right onto his dick. I took him into my mouth and fell to my knees to avoid falling in my 5"stilletos and to try and get better leverage. I licked and sucked his head until the entire shaft got hard and the veins popped out on it. I looked up at Evans face and he was staring right at me smiling like a Cheshire cat. He licked his lips and moaned a little but he never took his eyes off of me, not until I lowered my entire mouth onto his beautiful manhood. That's when he grabbed my head and began to pump himself into my mouth, face fucking me. I was so wrapped up into giving him the best head I could that I didn't even notice I had cum until it started running down my leg. I slurped and sucked and licked until eventually Evan rammed his dick all the way down my throat. I gagged hard mainly because I wasn't expecting him to be so aggressive. Honestly, it only turned me on more. Once we finally found our rhythm it wasn't long before Evan grabbed my head, let out a small moan and really rammed his dick down my throat. I felt him throbbing in my mouth so I knew he was about to cum. He came so hard in my mouth I thought I was going to choke to death. It filled up my mouth and made me gag. I had to wait until he eased himself out of my mouth before I even thought about attempting to swallow but I did it. I swallowed Evan's cum like a champ. I didn't want him thinking I was some weak ass chick or to weak or too prissy to swallow.

I didn't know what to think after that moment. Evan just sank down in the chair and started laughing. He laughed hysterically for about 30 seconds. Then he finally spoke to me. "Macy, turn around and take off your panties." OMG, I'm getting ready to get fucked by Evan Roberts! Nobody's ever going to believe this! Me, Macy Long! My reply to him, "I'm not wearing any sir."

The Sum of My Mistakes

Chapter Five

Evan

Oh shit! I can't believe this girl. She's more talented than I thought she would be. This shit feels so dam good. Freaky knows freaky so I'm glad I picked her to pleasure me. I can't believe she actually tried to kiss me. I guess that didn't go well for her. I wasn't going to fuck her but after that grand blow job performance I think she deserves the dick. See if she'll let me take her through the back door. That would really make me a happy guy. I love real freaky sex. The freakier the better. And I think Macy may be a real freaky ass freak. Ha, I'm in Heaven! Poor Saniya... if she was a good girl she could have been bent over on our dressing room table screaming my name, instead, she's home all alone while I'm getting ready to tear up this young tight pussy. "Oh shit Macy, you give phenomenal head. You didn't even flinch when I slid my stuff down your throat." "I hope you're not ready to leave yet. I'm not done with you."

"No Mr. Roberts, whatever you want I'm just here to please you."

No she didn't just tell me that! Now I'm really in heaven! Stand up Macy and turn around with your back to me." Let me stick this condom on, not trying to leave any evidence or make any babies. Not trying to get caught out there. "Macy, take your panties off"

"I'm not wearing any sir."

Oh My damn, she's trying to turn me out. "Bend over Macy, and spread those sexy legs of yours."

Macy did whatever I wanted her to do. She was a natural born freak. I did everything I could to Macy and she took it like a champ. Young girls are going to be the death of me.

I got done with Macy and we got into our cars and went our separate ways. I was kind of relieved the night was over. She was good to fuck but she was a little annoying, too eager and too willing. I like a bit of a challenge, some resistance or a little cat and mouse play. A female too willing and too able is a turn off.

I drove home nice and slow. I wanted to seize the moment for a few. I reached the house and opened the garage to park my car. Saniya's car was not in the garage. I parked my car and went into the house. "Saniya!" I called. I got no answer. I checked our bedroom and family room, no Saniya. I got straight on my phone and called her cell.

Ring...Ring...Ring...Ring... "You have reached Saniya; sorry I can't come to the phone right now, leave a message and I'll call you back as soon as I can."

"Damn!" I got her voicemail. Where in the hell is she?

The Sum of My Mistakes

Chapter Six

Saniya

I know he's out fucking that damn girl. I'm sick of sitting here waiting for Evan's ass to come home from whatever chick he's chosen for the night. This Macy chick is going to be a problem, I can feel it. Something not quite right about that girl. Well tonight instead of sitting around here feeling sorry for myself I think I'll go out for a little while. I can't just sit here looking stupid all night. Let me call my sister Jae'mi and see what she's doing tonight.

Ring....Ring....Ring....Ring...."Hello"

"Hey Saniya what's up?" Jae'mi answered. She sounded happy to hear from me.

"Hey Jae'mi, how are you?"

I'm good sis, how are you?"

"I'm good." I said, trying not to sound too down. "Jae'mi, what are you doing tonight?" I asked. I was hoping she felt like going out.

"I don't know yet, but it's my day off and I'm trying to get into something." Jae'mi said.

"Girl, I'm trying to get into something too... where do you want to go?" I asked my younger sister.

"Let's try that new club on Watchung Ave. Studio 44, I hear its nice inside, and it's so new the trifling negros hasn't had a chance to destroy it yet by fighting and shooting and acting all crazy over there."

"You are so right." I replied agreeing with Jae'mi.

"Plainfield is becoming so violent; you don't quite know where to hang out anymore. So many young people getting shot up and hurt, it's hard to go out and enjoy yourself." Jae'mi preached.

"Oh yeah girl, that's the truth." I said completely agreeing with her . I was hearing more and more about the crazy and violent it has been getting on the west end of town. Thank God we live on the East end in the Sleepy Hollow section of Plainfield.

"So are we going to hang out tonight sis?" Jae'mi asked, sounding excited.

"Hell yes!" I'm ready to go out and get my party on." I replied getting excited myself.

"So what are you wearing Saniya?"

"Something tight and sexy."

"Ooo girl Evan is going to have a fit you walking around like that!"

"Girl, fuck what Evan thinks, I'm going to wear what the hell I want to wear for a change!" I snapped.

"Damn girl, I didn't mean to get you all upset. I was just joking." "Is everything ok between you two?" Jae'mi asked

"Yeah girl you know how it is. Not every day is a good day when you're in a relationship. He just got on my nerves today." I said. Technically it wasn't a lie.

"Oh girl I'm sorry to hear that, what happened You know you can talk to me." Jae'mi said sounding genuinely concerned.

Oh no! What lie should I tell her? What story could I give that's as close to the truth as possible but doesn't have me coming out looking stupid? "Oh no girl, we just had a little disagreement, no big deal." I giggled. I feel bad lying to my sister, but I have to keep this secret to myself. I don't need my family coming down on me especially not now with all this nonsense with Evan.

"Ok girl, whatever you say." Jae'mi backed off with her questioning.

"What time do you want me to come pick you up Jae'mi?"

"Ummm... is 9 o'clock okay?"

"Yes that's perfect ha ha...Ok I will see you at 9. Bye."

Click.

"Whew! I dodged that bullet!" I said out loud. Look at me sitting here talking to myself. I'm not going to go crazy over this. I refuse. On the real, what am I going to do? I could always go back to dancing but at 37 years old, I'm not trying to get back on that pole. Although I still have the body for it. I'm absolutely not going back to the porn life. No way! I went through so much to get out of that life. Won't even consider going back, and besides, Azera is old enough to know what mommy is doing right now, and I don't want to embarrass her, or myself to be honest with you. I'm not going to fall back into a life that almost swallowed me whole. The porn life is not the way to go. It may seem glamorous and don't get me wrong, it is like a family. It's just like a dysfunctional family. I know Evan would never give me a job within his company even though I handle all of his business. I'm like a personal assistant to him. That would mean that I would have a little control over my life and Evan would never have that. I must figure out something though. Maybe I'll ask Sebastian if he knows anyone looking for help. I need enough money to move and sustain an apartment. In this economy jobs are few and far between. I've learned my lesson on finding a man who will take care of me. I always thought that this was what I wanted. Now that I have it, it's not what it appears.

Honestly, I'm so miserable. My man doesn't respect me, or himself. I spend most of my time alone, and although I want more children, Evan could care less. I long to be made love to, to connect with someone who desires me and who wants me not only sexually but on all levels. Evan is so selfish he's only out to please himself, all the damn time. After the life I've had, I need some pleasure, some real love and some healthy companionship. I know I started off handling life all wrong, at least I'm trying to get it together now. That doesn't mean I can't get into a little trouble and have just a little bit of fun.

Wow it's 8:30pm I need to hurry up and get in the shower and get dressed, I also want to leave before Evan gets home and tries to keep me from going out, I mean for once, it's finally all about me and I intend to have a great time out tonight.

The Sum of My Mistakes

Chapter Seven

Sebastian

I can't believe I'm stuck here living with my grandmother again. I've lost so much in the past few months, it's unbelievable. With this economy, I've lost many clients and so much money, I'm barely surviving. Child Support is kicking my ass on top of everything else. I'm a few hundred dollars behind, but not too much. I'm not trying to go to jail again. The last 3 year bid I did was enough for me.

If it wasn't for My Dear I'd be back in the streets. I'm going to have to figure something out. I can't keep going to My Dear getting loans that I can't pay back.

I definitely need this night out tonight. After the last few months I need a serious break. I'm going to get with my boys and go out and enjoy myself for once. I'm glad my boy Dante' is hooking me up tonight because of course my ass is broke again. He always helps me out when I'm in a bind. Dante' and I have been boys since kindergarten. He's watched me go through some shit. I'm grateful for the shit he does for me. He's a cool dude and I have much respect for him. I don't know where we're going tonight, but I can't wait to get there. It's been a while since I went out and had a good time. Since my life was shattered.

I heard the basement door open upstairs and I knew what was coming. "Sebastian, do you have my rent money?" My grandmother yelled from the upstairs kitchen door. "No My Dear." I yelled back from my apartment in the basement. Damn, I feel like shit telling her no again. My Dear has always been there for me when I needed her, and she should be. I took care of her when my grand pop died. Technically, she's just paying me back for what I did for her before. She'll get over me not having the money to pay her right now.

Again my grandmother yelled down the stairs for me. "Sebastian, come here and walk this dog for me please."

"Coming My Dear!" I yelled back up the stairs. I knew I had to tread lightly when it came to My Dear. She was getting pretty sick and tired of my excuses. I slowly walked up the basement stairs. I knew what was coming when I got to the top. "Sebastian, sit down for a minute, you and I need to talk." My Dear said as soon as I got to the top of the stairs. I did as I was told and sat down at my grandmother's kitchen table. I knew I was in for it. "Sebastian, it's been 2 months and you haven't had my money for rent."

"I know My Dear but..."

"No Sebastian, I don't want you to talk, I want you to listen." She interrupted.

"Yes ma'am." I replied. I knew I had to take this tongue lashing like a man. I sat in the chair closest to My Dear and took in everything she was saying to me. "Sebastian, what is the problem? How do you expect me to keep this mortgage paid if you're not contributing?" "I can't pay all of these bills by myself." she said her voice full of frustration.

"I know My Dear, I'm not doing this on purpose, and I'm just going through such a hard financial hit right now." I replied. She didn't want to

45

hear it.

"Sebastian, I understand that but I'm telling you now if you don't have the money by next week you're going to have to leave." Ouch that hurt. "I'm going to have to rent out that apartment and get some income coming in." "I understand My Dear." I mumbled. I knew it was coming and my time was almost up. I didn't even try to argue my case. I just gave My Dear a kiss on the cheek, faked a smile and told her thank you for everything. I also told her I understood and that was the end of the conversation.

After I returned from walking that damn dog, I got dressed to go out for the night. Dante' called me and told me to be ready by eight o'clock pm. Eight o'clock I was dressed and ready to go. Dante' swung by and picked me up. He had a few friends follow him over to my house. We all headed out to that new club Studio 44 on Watchung Ave in North Plainfield. Dante's friends pulled up behind us in front of the club. We were not too sure that we going to stay at that particular club, but I looked at all of the beautiful ladies going into the club and I knew I had to stay. Dante' agreed that the ladies were too fine to let them party alone so we found parking spaces across the street, parked and headed inside.

The Sum of My Mistakes

Chapter Eight

Saniya

"Wow this place must be packed, look at all these cars." "Jae'mi, come on girl, hurry up!"

"I'm coming; these new shoes are hurting my feet already!" Jae'mi complained.

"Ugh!" "Why would you wear a brand new pair of shoes out to a club without breaking them in first?" "That was stupid." I told Jae'mi.

"I know, I was trying to be cute, now I haven't even gotten to the door and I can feel my feet swelling up."

"Come on let's go back to the car, I have an extra pair of flats in my trunk that should fit you and go with your outfit."

"Thanks sis." Jae'mi said with a sign of relief on her face.

"No problem." I told my sister with a smile. I popped open my trunk and dug though the clothes and retrieved my flat black sandals and gave them to Jae'mi.

"Saniya, why do you have all of those clothes in your trunk?" Oh dam, I wasn't even thinking when I opened my trunk in front of my sister.

"I was giving this stuff away to the Red Cross." I lied.

"Saniya, stop lying to me, you always give me the stuff you don't want anymore and don't think I didn't notice that some of those things were brand new from our latest shopping trip." "What's going on sis?"

"I don't want to talk about it right now Jae'mi, I promise you I'll tell you everything tomorrow, right now I just want to unwind, party a little and maybe make a few new friends tonight. Is that cool?"

"Yes ma'am, it's cool with me." Jae'mi half smiled at me.

"Ok then, you ready now?"

"Yes I am!" Flashed a genuine smile at me.

"Okay then, let's go." I sang as I closed the trunk. Back to the club we headed.

Wow it is packed in here. I looked around at the crowd of partiers inside of Studio 44. It was a nice mix of people. Beautiful African American and Latino ladies. There were men in all shapes sizes and ethnicities. "Mmm, there are some fine brothers in here sis." I said to Jae'mi.

"Yes there are Saniya, but don't you already have a man?"

"Not tonight I don't!" I laughed and then I gave my sister a high five. I came across this one brother, Mmm mm mm. Tall, chocolate and fine as hell. He would put Evan to shame. I love a fine man. I can't resist them. I love them tall, 6' and higher. The taller the better. I love all shades of African American. I like them very handsome, with goatees or completely smooth skin and pretty smiles are everything to me. I get really weak for a pretty smile. Don't get me wrong, I love and have dated men of all cultures, I just prefer my beautiful black men.

"Ooo two seats just opened at the bar, let's go get them Jae'mi." Jae'mi rushed over to the two seats and sat down in one of them and placed her purse in the other seat. I took my time getting over to the bar. I wanted to watch all of the beautiful people that were there tonight. I wanted to see each and every person that was there just in case my Mr. Right was in the building. I was determined to meet him tonight no matter what. I would explain my behavior to my sister tomorrow but tonight it was all about me.

I sat down at the bar and ordered myself a glass of Moscato. My sister ordered the same and after receiving our drinks, we both turned our chairs around to look at the crowd. That's when I noticed my former personal trainer Sebastian sitting at a table with three really nice looking guys. Sebastian looked so handsome. I always see him in his trainer outfits and he was always down to business when I got there. I've never see him in dress clothes. It was nice to see him dressed up and in a social setting.

"Hey Saniya, who are you staring at?" Jae'mi asked.

"Oh no I'm not staring, I see my old trainer Sebastian sitting over there at that table with those four guys.

"Which one?" Jae'mi asked hoping it was the very fine chocolate brother sitting with a group of equally handsome men.

"He's the light skinned brother with the hazel eyes and curly black hair." I said trying not to look too obvious. "Saniya, he is gorgeous!" Jae'mi admitted. I've never really looked at Sebastian like that. I'm not blind, I can see he's a good looking man, and there was something very different about the way he looked tonight.

I kept my cool and just shrugged my shoulders at Jae'mi's awe of Sebastian. I turned around to face the bartender to order another glass of

Moscato and Jae'mi started tapping me on my shoulder hysterically. "He's coming over here Saniya. "Ooo can you introduce me to him please!" I hated it when my little sister squealed like a little piglet. I slowly turned around to see Sebastian walking straight towards us. Damn! He really is fine as hell, I thought to myself as he approached. "Hey Saniya, how are you?" Sebastian said to me with a big smile on his face.

"Hey Sebastian, how are you?" I said playing it cool.

"I'm great lady; it's good to see you." Sebastian hugged me as he spoke. Damn he smelled so good. I almost forgot where I was for a minute. I got lost in his hug.

"Good to see you too." I replied smiling to myself. I got myself together and introduced him to my sister."Oh, Sebastian, this is my little sister Jae'mi, Jae.mi, this is Sebastian my former personal trainer." --"And I hope also your friend." he interrupted.

"Oh of course, we're friends Sebastian that goes without saying." I agreed.

"Nice to meet you Sebastian." Jae'mi said with a huge smile and nothing but seduction in her voice. My sister is a sweetheart, but when it comes to men she's like a teenager. I was so tickled by her behavior I even giggled to myself. My sister is absolutely beautiful, but she was the worst at flirting.

"Nice to meet you too Jae'mi." "You're just as beautiful as your sister." Sebastian said.

"Thank you." Jae'mi said with an even bigger smile now on her face. I think I actually blushed when he said that.

"Awww... thank you Sebastian." I said before I even had a chance to stop myself.

"Saniya, may I buy you and your sister a drink?"

"Well, we just got these, maybe in a few minutes after we're done with these drinks."

"Ok, well at least promise me you'll dance with me before the night is out Saniya."

"Sure Sebastian." I agreed. I wanted to run out to the dance floor with Sebastian but I kept it cool.

"Ok, I'll be back in a few minutes to get you, Jae'mi, again, very nice to meet you." Sebastian said as he flashed another huge smile on his face. Damn he has a nice smile, I thought to myself as Sebastian walked away.

"Oh my Gosh Saniya, he is SO fine!" Jae'mi squealed again.

"Calm down Jae'mi." Yes he is, I thought to myself. Really fine.

The rest of the night went very well for both me and Jae'mi. We partied and sipped Moscato until 1:30am when they announced last call at the bar. In the few hours we had been at the club, we had the most fun we've had in years. Jae'mi had a chance to meet Mr. Chocolate whose real name is Dante' Moore one of Newark's finest. The other two gentlemen were brothers Charles and Robert Lane, who were also personal trainers.

Sebastian and I danced most of the night together. He dances his ass off and I don't do too bad myself. Dante and Jae'mi danced together and Charles and Robert ended up meeting a few seemingly nice young ladies sitting at the table next to them. Finally the lights came on and everyone began to file out of the club. Sebastian grabbed my hand and asked me if he could walk us to our car. Of course I said yes and all of us headed to the parking lot across the street from the club. Once we all reached the car, Jae'mi and Dante' exchanged numbers and hugs, Sebastian and I agreed to call each other and for me to get back into the gym. Sebastian opened his arms to give me a hug and I walked into his arms and placed my hands around his waist. He wrapped his arms around me and held me for a few seconds. He held me like he didn't want to let me go. Suddenly my phone began to ring. We broke our embrace and I retrieved my phone from my purse. Evan's name and picture flashed across the screen. I hadn't thought about Evan or what was going on with us all night. I hit the ignore button on my phone and threw the phone back into my purse. Sebastian quickly noticed the look on my face and asked me was everything ok. "No not really." I said with my head down.

"Well if you need to talk Saniya, I'm always willing to listen." Then he flashed that beautiful smile again.

"I may take you up on that offer" I said then flashed a big smile of my own. My phone beeped twice signaling I had a voice message. I pressed the "OK" button and once again threw the phone back into my purse.

"Saniya, why don't we all head out to IHOP or the Union Diner and have some breakfast, I'm starving Jae'mi asked me with a big shit eating grin on her face. I was hungry also, so I agreed that we would go to get something to eat.

"Would you mind if we joined you?" Sebastian asked.

"I don't mind at all" I said quickly.

"Hey fellas you all want to go to IHOP or the diner in Union to grab something to eat?" Sebastian asked his boys. Everyone replied yes, including the two young ladies that were talking to Charles and Robert. So we all got into our cars and headed out to Rt. 22 to go to the Union Diner.

Once in the car I checked out my phone to see if I had missed any calls. 4 missed calls from Evan and 4 voicemails. I had 1 text message, also from Evan. The text message said "Where the fuck are you?" and was left at 1:42a.m. Only 20 minutes ago. You mean to tell me this asshole just got home and realized I wasn't there? That means his ass has been out all night without a care or concern for me I thought to myself. Now I was getting upset all over again. I pressed the button to dial my voicemail and this was the first message I heard... "Saniya, where the hell are you?" that message was left at 1:43a.m. I pressed number 7 to erase that message and then the second message played. "Saniya, I'm not in the mood for these petty games, get your ass home NOW!" That message was left at 1:45a.m. I immediately pressed number 7 again to erase. Then the third message played: "I'm not fucking playing with your ass Saniya, answer this fucking phone!" That message was left at 1:55 a.m. I smiled and then pressed 7 once again to delete. Fourth message: "Saniya, you fucking whore, I don't know where the fuck you are, but...I pressed 7 to erase, not wanting to hear the rest of the message. "Did he call you a whore?" Jae'mi's voice snapped me out of the shock I was in. "Saniya what in the hell is going on?" I know that arrogant asshole did not call you a whore!" Jae'mi yelled. "Jae'mi, I told you I will talk to you tomorrow about it."

55

"I want to talk about it now!" Jae'mi yelled again.

"Dammit Jae'mi, stop yelling at me, I got enough of that shit earlier from Evan. I promise you, I will explain everything to you, just do me a favor, don't mention any of this to anyone. Let's just go to the diner, enjoy ourselves for a little while longer tonight and I will deal with Evan when I get home."

"Okay sis, Jae'mi said after a few seconds of hesitation.

"Oh cool, we're here" I said to change the subject.

"Yay!!!!" Jae'mi cheered. Now let's go in and have a few laughs."

"Yes, let's", I said laughing with my sister. So glad my night wasn't over yet.

The Sum of My Mistakes

Chapter Nine

Evan

I called this bitch 4 times and got voicemail every time. What the hell? I can't believe I get home and she's not here. She gets on my damn nerves. Where in the hell could she have possibly gone? It looks like some of her clothes are gone. I should just take my ass to bed and change the locks in the morning. That will teach her ass not to call herself leaving me. I have work in the morning; I don't have time for this bullshit. Now if she came back home tonight and I was gone again, then what in the hell would she have to say. You know I swore I would never put my hands on a woman, and I'm going to try my best not to knock the shit out of her when she does get here, but she's really pushing my buttons. I have a whole lot of shit on my mind and I'm not about to take this shit from Saniya. You know, you really can't turn a whore into a housewife. I get caught a few times getting some head and here she goes trying to leave. What the hell is wrong with women? They're always on some bullshit.

I should call Macy and see if she's still up. Maybe I'll go back to my office building and tear her ass up again. I don't like to stay with one extra chick too long or be with them too often but Macy is a serious freak and I like that.

Man, I'm so stressed out I don't know what to do. All of this bullshit with Saniya, financial problems with the house and the business. Ex-wife/baby mama drama. It's just too much shit going on. I wish Saniya would fucking understand that. No, she wants to argue with me over some trick. Speaking of tricks let me call Macy's ass. Ring....ring.... Hello. "What's up Macy, you sleep?"

"No, I'm not sleep Evan."

"I thought I wore your little ass out tonight."

"Ha ha... yes you did, I really enjoyed myself Evan."

"Cool, what are you doing now? You want to meet me back at my office?"

"Sure Evan, you want me to leave now?"

"No not right now, just give me a few minutes; I have to take care of something first ok Macy? It's 4:30.a.m. now, I'll call you back in a few minutes, try not to fall asleep."

"Okay." Click.

Do I hear the garage door opening? Hell yeah, just wait until Saniya gets her ass into this house!

"Where in the fuck have you been Saniya? It's almost 5:00 in the morning!"

"Evan, not tonight." Saniya had the nerve to say to me.

"What in the hell do you mean Evan not tonight! Who in the hell are you talking to Saniya and why in the hell do you smell like gas?!"

"Evan, stop trying to start a fight with me every 5 fucking minutes! I went out to Studio 44 with Jae'mi, we went to the Union Diner after the club, and we ran out of gas over on South Ave by the KFC. I had to walk over to the Shell station to get gas and put it in the car. I did that, I dropped Jae'mi off and now I'm home...Shit!" Saniya yelled. "Where the fuck was you Evan? How's that bitch Macy doing tonight? Does she fuck

59

as well as she gives blowjobs?" Saniya spat.

Damn, I feel stupid, but instead of letting this argument go, I had to make my point. "Shut the fuck up Saniya, I wasn't with no damn Macy, I lied. I went to have a little drink and clear my mind."

"Whatever Evan, I'm going to take a shower and go to bed in the extra bedroom, goodnight." With that said, Saniya disappeared up the dark stairs. Instead of trying to continue this argument, I just put my phone on vibrate and headed to bed myself. I'm just too tired for all this drama. Besides, I was honestly relieved that Saniya was home. I seriously thought she left me for good this time.

Damn I can't sleep. I'm tired as hell but I just can't sleep tonight too much shit on my mind. Damn! Its 7:00 in the morning and all I've done was toss and turn all night. I checked in on Saniya and she's knocked out. Lucky her. Macy called my phone 6 times since 5:30a.m. I'll be sure to set her ass straight when I see her later today. I don't play that psycho stalker bullshit. My ladies know their place and they know I don't play that calling me when you feel like it shit. Everybody knows my situation and they get at me when I want to see them, not vice versa. I can see now that Mrs. Macy Long is going to be a serious problem. So, let me get my ass up and get ready for work and for my little talk with Macy's ass. Buzz.... Buzz....

Buzz....Buzz.... Dam crazy bitch calling me again! Now I'm pissed off and

I let her know when I answered the phone. "What!!?"

"Hi Evan, it's me Macy." "I just wanted"....

"Macy, why in the hell do you keep calling me?" "Well Evan, you never

called me back after our talk at 4:30 this morning."

"Well Macy, If I didn't call you back that means that I must have changed

my mind." That doesn't give you the wear with all to call me over and over

and over again all damn night long! Do you understand me Macy?"

"I'm sorry Evan; I was just concerned about you when I didn't hear from

you again."

"Well, my lady got home and it was time for me to spend some time with

her.

"Oh, I'm so sorry Evan; I really didn't mean to upset you by calling so

much."

"Macy, look I will call you when I want to see you. I will call you; don't

call me especially all times of the night."

"Again I'm sorry Evan."

"Yeah, ok I have to go get ready for work. Good bye Macy."

"Good bye Evan." Click. Here we go with that young girl mentality. See, I don't have the patience for this. I have too much on my mind for a whole bunch of foolishness. I'm just trying to get in it and get out, no feelings and no emotions and no bullshit.

I took my phone off of vibrate and put the ringer back on. Then I decided to go look in on Saniya before I got ready for work. I stood up to go into the other room and took a long look at myself in the tall mirror in the hallway. More dark circles were forming under my eyes and now my eyes are bloodshot red from not sleeping last night. I see more of these damn lines forming around my eyes and my mouth today than there were yesterday morning. I feel tired and depressed. "What in the hell is going on with my life?" I said to myself.

I made my way down to the hallway to check on Saniya. I slowly and quietly opened the door to the guest room where Saniya slept last night. She was still knocked out. "Damn you're beautiful." I whispered to her hoping my voice would wake her up. She didn't budge. Right then I decided I would be late for work today. I wanted to make Saniya a nice breakfast in bed and serve it to her. Whatever anger I felt the past few days has dissipated and right now all I want is to hold my baby and tell her how much I love her. Ring... Ring... Ring... Dam my phone is ringing. That better not be Macy's ass. Ring...Ring.....Ring... I don't recognize this number. "Hello" "Is this Mr. Evan Roberts?"

"Yes this is Mr. Evan Roberts who may I ask is calling?"

"This is Deputy Chief Aaron Smith Plainfield Fire Department. Mr. Roberts I need you to meet me at your property on South Avenue in Plainfield."

"What's the problem Deputy Smith?" "

Sir, I'm sorry to inform you that your building is involved in a fire."

"WHAT!?" Oh no!!" "I'll be right there Deputy Smith." Click. I ran back into the other room. "Saniya! Wake up!"

"Wha...what's wrong Evan? Why are you yelling?"

"Saniya our South Avenue location is on fire!"

"What?!"

"I just got a call from Deputy Chief Smith from Plainfield Fire Department who informed me that the store was on fire!"

"Oh no Evan!"

"Hurry up and get dressed!"

"Okay, okay, I'm getting dressed right now."

"Please hurry up Saniya."

"Evan, everything's going to be Ok, calm down."

"Saniya, I can't calm down, everything that can go wrong is going wrong!"

"I know Evan, but it will all be ok." Saniya was always so positive. I can't explain why I do the things I do to her. I guess I am as much of an asshole as everyone thinks I am. All I know now right now is I need to get my ass to the store and find out what's going on.

Saniya and I tore down our driveway and screeched to a stop at the stop sign on our block and Terrell Rd. We made a left down Terrell road straight to South Ave. Made another left down South Ave to Leland. Crossed Leland Ave. and got to Woodland and South Ave. where we were stopped by the police officer who was blocking the road with his police car. I parked the car and Saniya and I went running down South Ave. as far as the Fire department would let me go. There I saw part of my life burn before my very eyes. Flames were shooting out of the building windows and the fire department appeared to be really fighting the blaze but the blaze was winning. There were fire departments from Plainfield, North Plainfield, South Plainfield and Watchung fighting the fire. I was so focused on the fire I never noticed that Saniya was no longer by my side. I looked around the crowd that was standing across the street from my burning building for her, but I didn't see her. Then I noticed something out of the corner of my eye. There was Macy standing in the crowd. What in the hell is she doing here? I thought to myself. She's supposed to be at work at my main building in Newark. Not only that, but how did she hear about the fire quickly enough to be here while it was still burning, she didn't even live in the area. Mental note to myself, written reprimand for Macy for being late to work. I'd love to fire her, but after what happened last night, I would have a hell of a law suit on my hands. I don't know what that girl was thinking, but I don't play when it comes to my business. She's very lucky. My thoughts went back to Saniya and the fact that she was nowhere to be found all of a sudden. I wondered if she saw Macy standing in that crowd and decided this was all too much for her. All of a sudden I felt something. I don't know what the hell it was but something in my gut. No, Saniya wouldn't do this. I knew I had to shake that feeling and handle my business. I asked the nearest fireman where I could find Deputy Chief Smith and he pointed to the fireman standing next to a table with various papers and binders sitting on it. Deputy Chief Smith was standing next to a few other firemen and what looked to be some police officers. I introduced myself and shook Deputy Chief Smith's hand. "Deputy Smith, it's a pleasure meeting you, how is everything looking in there? Did anyone get hurt? Was there anyone in the building at the time of the fire?" I was firing questions so fast myself that I didn't notice the look on their faces. Then Deputy Chief Smith began to fire his own questions.

"Mr. Roberts, We're still trying to put this very difficult fire out. Can you tell me if there are any hazardous materials in your store?"

"No sir, I answered.

"Mr. Roberts, can you tell me if anyone has any kind of vendetta against you?" It took me a moment to answer that question. I put my head down and took a second to think of everyone that may have something against me. The list was so long and included Saniya so I just replied with a weak "No". That's when I noticed that Saniya had taken a position to my right. I tried to grab her hand and introduce her, but she quickly but subtly snatched her hand away. I was privately embarrassed, but I knew I had to deal with that later. I introduced her despite her behavior. "Deputy Chief, this is my girlfriend Saniya Wheeler. I continued to pay attention and answer Deputy Chief Smith's questions; I just thought his questions were a bit unnecessary.

"Mr. Roberts, are you able to supply your whereabouts between 4 am and 6am?" The officer standing next to the Deputy Chief asked me.

66

"I was home officer." I replied. Why would he ask me that? I thought to myself. Finally Deputy Chief Smith finally admitted what had popped into my head just seconds before. "Mr. Roberts, this fire was definitely arson" he said to me with a look of suspicion. His facial expressions told it all, I was his number one suspect in an arson that I didn't commit. Saniya tapped me on my shoulder and said she was going to call the insurance company and tell them what was going on. Saniya was so good at keeping up relationships with me as far as my business was concerned. Insurance company, my bank, my creditors, and even my staff. She was part of the reason I hired Macy. Damn, speaking of Macy let me call my Newark location and make sure there is someone there taking care of things at that location. I glanced back into the crowd to see if I saw Macy's ass still standing out there. Thank God, she' wasn't there anymore. I hope she took her stupid ass to work. Here comes that feeling again, something's just not right about that girl. "Evan, Evan!" Saniya yelled as she was running up to me with a look of horror on her face.

"What's wrong Saniya?" "Jerry from our Newark location just called me and the police department just walked in looking for you."

"Looking for me for what?"

"Wait, Evan, he's putting them on the phone now." "Yes, sir he's right here." Saniya said to the person on the other end of the phone. At the same time Saniya handed me the phone a Plainfield Police Officer approached me and asked me what my name was. "Evan Roberts sir, is everything ok officer?"

"Mr. Roberts, my name is Officer Ford, Plainfield Police Department, Mr. Roberts; we have a warrant for your arrest "For what sir?"

"Sexual battery please put your hands behind your back sir."

The Sum of My Mistakes

Chapter Ten

Macy

I can't believe Evan yelled at me like that. He has a lot of nerve correcting me. He pursued me. He approached me. I didn't start this relationship he did. I'm not one to fuck with. I will make Evan's life hell. He has no idea who he's messing with. I bet when he gets that phone call about his store being on fire he will think about how the hell he talked to me. I will call him when I want for whatever I want. I don't give a shit about that bitch he lives with. Shit, he doesn't care about her ass, why should I? I haven't had many relationships but one thing a man cannot do is tell me what to do. My parents couldn't tell me what to do. Once I get him where I want him, things with him and that girl are going to be over anyway. I will get rid of her ass soon enough.

I had to go back to the fire. I couldn't wait to see Evan. He's going to be a little busy today after all of the work I did this morning. Since last night I miss him so much. I know he's going to need my love and comfort after this is all over, but that's just how it goes when you piss me off. Anyway, last night was magical. Evan fucked me so good I never want another man. Only love could be made with our actions last night. Giving him the blowjob was great but fucking him was beyond fantastic. It first started when he bent me over the desk. Evan entered me from behind hard. I spread my legs apart and he slid his dick right inside of me. He grabbed my neck and my waist to balance himself. He stroked me so hard I almost flew over the desk. Being small girl men can lift me up and put me wherever they want. Once we got deep into it, he lifted me up with his strong arms and actually bounced me off and on his dick. Then the ultimate happened. Evan laid me on the desk, put my head as far down as it would go and I arched my back and put my ass up as far as it would go. Then it happened he entered my ass. It hurt like hell at first but once we got our rhythm it felt so good I came over and over and over again. He kissed my neck and nibbled hard on my back. I looked in the mirror and he left beautiful passion marks all over me. You can actually mistake them for bruises. He's so nasty and freaky like me. For a 50 year old man he's so great sexually. He really turned me out almost literally. We made love for hours. He didn't really talk to me too much but he dug himself into me like I was the only woman he ever wanted. Last night Evan became mine. All mine. Nobody has ever made love to me like that and I will never let him go, EVER! I can't wait to be Mrs. Macy Roberts.

Now I had to go to the South Ave. location and see some of my handy work. Evan won't realize I really did him a huge favor until after he calms down. I know he must be furious right now. Good thing is if he thinks Saniya set fire to his store he's sure to leave her for good. Now the sexual battery story, well that's just to teach him a lesson about talking to me like that. Glad I didn't take a shower after our love making. Now the police have everything they need to arrest and charge Evan with Sexual battery. I hate to do it to him but I need him to need me. I know Saniya won't stand by his side after this and I'll have him exactly where I want him. I'll tell him I'll drop all charges if he agrees to dump Saniya and then we'll be together. It's that simple.

Ring....Ring... Ring.... Ring.... Who the hell is this calling me? Why is Evan's name flashing across my screen? He was arrested already and I know he didn't make bail that quickly. "Hello?" "

"Macy, this is Saniya."

"What do you want Saniya?"

"Good job genius, but you must know Evan's going to break your neck when I bail him out."

"Whatever bitch!"

"LOL! Little girl, you picked the right one, you should've stayed out of grown folk's business Macy."

"Saniya I am grown and what Evan did to me was wrong, how can you call me and talk to me like this?" I yelled and began to fake cry hysterically, just in case she was recording our conversation. I had to play this to the end.

"Whatever Macy, you didn't look like you were being abused when I caught you with his dick in your mouth. You should have thought this through before you started it. This may bring Evan and me even closer."

"Shut the fuck up you stupid bitch!" I spat at Saniya. How dare she call me and talk to me this way! I was a victim and as far as her and Evan becoming closer, I'll kill that bitch first. Evan was going to be mine by any means necessary.

"Have a good day Macy and remember the truth shall set you free!" Saniya sang into the phone. I immediately hung up the phone on that fat bitch. I did think it through. I thought long and hard about what I was going to do to get Evan all to myself. She's lucky I didn't resort to plan B, killing her ass. If I know my Evan, he had insurance on the building in Plainfield and he'll even thank me for helping him get a nice payoff. I feel sorry for the people that work there, but they'll find other jobs. Now Evan will have to work completely out of the Newark building once he gets out of jail. He's a very wealthy man so I know he'll be able to bail himself out. Then he'll call me. He has to call me. I'm all he has right now.

Hours have gone by and no call from Evan. It's five in the afternoon and still nothing. Maybe Saniya is right. Maybe I didn't think this through. Her ass should have been in jail too today, but she called me. What the hell is going on? Other than the phone call about them arresting Evan, my phone didn't ring all day and that's just strange. Not even my job, nobody called me today. I'm scared to call Evan; the police might be monitoring his phone calls. Bang! bang!, bang! "Who the hell is banging on my door?" "Who is it?" I yelled at the door.

"Police Mrs. Long, Open the door please!" I looked out of my window to see three officers standing in front of the door. I slowly opened the door to find three police officers standing there. They didn't look like Newark officers though. I slowly opened my door for the officers. Two male officers and one female. "Yes, how can I help you officers?"

The Sum of My Mistakes

Chapter Eleven

Saniya

No, this dumb bitch didn't! No she did not! Ha ha ha... I hate to laugh, but Karma is a bitch! The look on Evan's face when they put those handcuffs on him was priceless! I actually sat for a little while thinking about how I could get back at him for hurting me and disrespecting me. Glad I prayed on it instead of acting on anger. Now I can't believe I'm sitting here at the police department waiting to bail Evan out and for them to release him from jail. He's lucky I was with him when they arrested him. I shouldn't have but I was able to explain to the police about Evan's "relationship" with Macy. Evan is the biggest asshole I know, but he's not a rapist. I guess his little lie about not being with her last night came to bite him on the ass. I wonder what happened last night for her to accuse him of sexual battery. I know Evan and his rough sexual moments. We have both awaken in the morning all bruised up because of our love making. This does tell me one thing, There's no way in hell that I can stay with Evan. Not after this and not after the wonderful time I had with Sebastian last night. Wow, what a difference a day makes.

I've been here all damn day. I need to go home, take a shower and get refreshed. Oh great I see one of the officers from the fire. "Excuse me may I please speak to that officer that just walked by the window." I asked the officer sitting at the desk by the window.

"Sure ma'am, let me get him for you." The short cute Police Officer at the desk walked over and asked the officer to come to the window and speak to me for a minute. "How may I help you miss?" I didn't really notice when I was at the fire scene, but this officer was really handsome. Tall, light skinned gentleman not too big, not to thin, actually pretty perfect. With big brown eyes and nice teeth. The tag on his uniform said D. Long.

"Officer Long, I'm so sorry to bother you, but did they ever get the fire under control on South Ave.?" I asked him.

"Yes they did miss, he replied.

"Oh good I said and thank you."

"Sure, no problem" he replied.

"They are still out on the fire scene if you'd like to go back and talk to the firemen." he said before he turned around to go back behind the big wooden door.

"Oh ok good. I said to him now with a little bit of a smile on my face.

"Excuse me officer, may I ask you one more question before you leave?"

"Sure ma'am."

"This is a little personal, so can you come out here so I can ask you in private please." Officer Long followed me out of the lobby area and into another area right outside of the main entry doors. "Officer Long, do you know a woman named Macy Long?" Officer Long's entire facial expression changed.

"Unfortunately yes I do. She's my soon to be ex-wife" he said with a painful look in his eyes.

"Miss I don't know who you are or why you're asking me these questions, but if she's a friend of yours, watch yourself. Macy has some serious issues."

"She's not my friend by a long shot" I said and then I put my head down. Once again it hit me that she and Evan had slept together last night.

"Miss....I'm sorry, I didn't introduce myself, and my name is Saniya, Saniya Wheeler."

"Nice to meet you Saniya, I'm Dayton, Dayton Long."

"Nice to meet you too Dayton." I said finally smiling.

"Well Saniya if Macy's giving you any trouble, here's my card. Please feel free to call me anytime. Macy has a lot of mental issues and she's capable of just about anything." Dayton said this with a very serious expression on his face.

"Is she capable of filing false rape charges on someone?"

"Oh, is that your husband in the booking area? The one getting ready to be taken to Newark police department?" Officer Long asked.

"He's not my husband, he's my ex-boyfriend and yes, he was arrested for sexual battery."

"Is Macy his accuser?"

"Yes she is, but I'm positive he didn't sexually abuse or rape her, I'd bet my life on it, and what do you mean they are getting ready to take him to Newark?"

"His charges are out of Newark not Plainfield, so we have to transport him to Newark tonight."

"So you mean he's not going to be able to be bailed out?"

"I don't think so Ms. Wheeler, but let me go check for you."

"Ok thank you." and with that Officer Dayton Long disappeared behind the heavy wooden door where I wasn't allowed. "Wow, Macy's husband." I said out loud. "He seems like such a nice guy, how did he get stuck with Macy as a wife? I thought to myself. Boy, if Evan has to be stuck in jail all night he's going to have a complete fit. Good for his ass. Maybe next time he decides to cheat on someone, he'll think twice about it. All of this nonsense over some ass. I wonder was it worth it to him.

Buzz...Buzz...Buzz. "Ooo my phone"...I scrambled through my purse searching for my cell phone. Sebastian's name flashed across the screen. "Hello."

"Hey beautiful, I was just calling to see how your day went today."

"Hey Sebastian honestly it was a day from hell."

"Oh, I'm so sorry to hear that Saniya. You know if you need to talk I'm right here for you."

"Aww Thanks Sebastian"

"Hey Saniya, how about dinner tonight?"

I had to think about that. Hmmm I wondered if it was too early to go on a date. F it, why not go? I thought to myself. "Dinner would be wonderful Sebastian."

"Well it's 6p.m. now, how about 8 o'clock?" Sebasian sounded anxious.

"8 is cool. Where would you like to meet Sebastian?" I didn't want him to know where we lived.

"How about Ariang's on Rt. 22 in Mountainside?" "

Umm, how about somewhere else?" I didn't want to go there, that was Evan's and my spot.

"Ok you pick the spot then." Sebastian said.

"How about we meet up at Friday's in Union?"

"Sounds like a plan to me." Sebastian said that with so much enthusiasm. It felt good to finally feel appreciated.

"Ok, see you at 8 o'clock Sebastian."

"Ok, bye Saniya."

"Bye." I said and then I hung up. Wow! I have a date with Sebastian!"

"Excuse me Ms. Wheeler." Officer Long's voice jolted me back to reality.

"Yes, I'm sorry Officer Long."

"Just letting you know that Mr. Roberts is not going to be released this evening." "Ok, so what do I do now?" "Just let me speak to the prosecutor tomorrow morning and I'll see what I can do to help you guys out."

"Thank you, Officer Long."

"No, please call me Dayton." "Thank you Dayton."

"You're welcome Saniya, is it ok for me to call you Saniya?" He said with a huge smile on his face. Is he flirting with me? I thought to myself.

"Yes of course you can call me Saniya."

"Give me a call tomorrow morning around 9 o'clock, and I'll let you know what your options are from there."

"Thank you Dayton."

"You're welcome Saniya."

"Well, have a good night."

"You have a good night also Saniya; hopefully I'll see you tomorrow." I smiled back at Officer Dayton Long and waved a little goodbye. Yes, me too I thought to myself. "How in the hell did a girl like Macy get to marry a guy like him? I was definitely going to find out.

The Sum of My Mistakes

Chapter Twelve

Evan

I cannot believe this bullshit. I'm actually stuck in jail on some trumped up charges. I've never been to jail a day in my life. It's horrible in here. That dam Macy is going to regret the day she met me. I can't believe that bitch lied on me like this. I just want to go home, kiss Saniya and Azera, tell Saniya how much I love her, hope she forgives me, and go on with my life. I made such a mistake messing around with that young stupid girl, now I'm stuck here in jail and that crazy bitch is home, but not for long. Apparently she has a warrant for her arrest for nonpayment of child support. She's going to have a very unpleasant surprise coming to her any minute now, thanks to Officer Dayton Long. I can't believe he was married to Macy. He told me Macy left him and their 4 month old daughter a few months ago. Now he's a single father and this girl is running wild. I never really had a conversation with Macy. I never asked her anything about herself nor did I ever plan on doing so. Now I find out that she's trifling as hell, extremely immature and a dead beat mother. I guess I don't need to talk. I'm a grown ass man, I don't see my kids, I messed around on Saniya and my ex-wife. Here I am messing around with Macy and I should have known better. I just wanted some ass. No commitment, no conversation, just a good blow job and some ass. Macy gave me both. Now it's going to take a lot of money and some prayer to get me out of this mess. I'm glad I have enough money to fight these charges, but this shit is crazy. The ass was good as hell, but it wasn't worth all of this. I got no sleep last night and I'm beyond tired and I can't sleep in this nasty place.

On top of these charges, I can't believe my Plainfield store was burned down. I'm glad I had enough sense to have good insurance. Hopefully this whole arson thing won't mess my insurance claim up. Deputy Chief Smith says the fire was definitely arson. Once the arson investigator finishes his investigation, I can move forward with the insurance company. Once they prove that it wasn't me who set the fire, the insurance company shouldn't have a problem paying my claim. I can rebuild the store and give everyone their jobs back. I hope Saniya starts the procedure tomorrow if not tonight. I can't even go to the property and check out all of the damage, because I'm stuck here in this hell hole. Now they're talking about me having to go to Newark Police Department in Essex County. That's where Macy filed the charges. That crazy chick told them I made her do all of the things we did last night. Apparently she had a bunch of bruises on her body from the crazy sex we had last night. I will admit, I was hitting that shit hard as hell, but I didn't sexually assault her. I would never do that to a woman. Thank God my property has cameras in the parking lot and throughout the hallways and in the store area. I kind of wish I had cameras in that empty office so everyone could see the truth about what happen last night. Stupid bitch didn't realize she was being taped as we arrived and when we left and you can see her all hugged up on me as we were leaving. Not one sign of fear was in her face when we left my building. After the detectives retrieve the DVD's, I should be released or at least given a bail.

I don't know what to think about Saniya coming home smelling like gas this morning. Would she burn down my store just to get back at me for cheating on her? Is she that petty and evil? Also, where the hell did she run off to when we were at the fire scene? All of those employees are going to need their pay at least for the next few weeks. That's even more money out of my pocket. I'm so glad I'm able to provide money for them to cover their pay for a while. I'll have one of the ladies replace Macy in Newark and the other do some office work for me. The young man Eli my part time stock person I'll check my connections and see if I can get him another part time job until I rebuild. Macy will definitely be fired immediately. That firing will have to come from someone other than myself. I'll have Luke my GM handle that so we won't end up with another lawsuit. Now that that's all going to be handled, what in the hell was Macy doing at the fire scene? How did she get from the police department to the fire scene that quick? Maybe that bitch knew they would arrest me there and she wanted to see me go to jail? When in the hell did she file charges against me? I spoke to her at 6 something this morning and they arrested me at 10:00 am. I know they have to do rape kits and examinations and stuff, how did she do all of that in such a small amount of time?

Officer Long says he's going to let me know the time line when all the charges were filed. I appreciate that brother's help. This is all too much for me to swallow. I know Karma is a bitch, but damn! I guess this is what my life has come to. I guess I've been so busy running around and doing me I haven't been paying enough attention to other people's shit. All the women I've slept with, trying not to pay my ex-wife her alimony, not going to see my kids. To be honest, I wouldn't blame Saniya if she did burn down the store. People think I don't give a shit most of the time, but I do care. I care what happens to Saniya, more than what I've been able to show her, my kids, and even my ex-wife. Once I get out of here tomorrow, I'm going to sit Saniya down and apologize to her. Tell my accountant to send my ex her alimony and try to convince her to sit down to dinner with me so I can make arrangements to see my kids. I owe her a big apology and an explanation. I have to think about what I'm going to say to everyone. I've done a lot of shit to everyone who cares about me in the past 3 months. Ever since I spoke to him. I can't even explain why I've done the things I've done, or what's going through my head. All I know is I have to make all of this right. The only thing that continues to bother me is that damn gasoline smell Saniya had on her when she got home this morning. I can't think of anyone else who I've pissed off that much. What if she did burn down the store? What will I do then? Do I turn her in or keep it to myself? Then there's the matter of the little conversation I had 3 months ago that changed my life and really made me think about my worth as a man. He really messed my life up. I've been unable to love a woman, unable to feel what it's like to really be loved. Or get close to my kids. All because of him. Maybe I should tell Saniya about him, about how my life changed when I spoke to the man I've been longing for my entire life. Maybe I should just tell everyone the fucking truth.

The Sum of My Mistakes

Chapter Thirteen

Sebastian

Saniya Wheeler. Mmm mm mm. That will be the ultimate betrayal to sleep with Saniya. Evan's ass thought he was big shit fucking around with my girl. I wonder how he's going to feel to have it done to him. Saniya is a beautiful girl. I don't see how Evan's old ass got her in the first place. Sexy ass Saniya "Sweet Serenity." I've seen all of her porn movies and I remember the first time I saw her dance a few years ago in New York. I wanted her bad as hell then and I still want her bad as hell. Now's my chance to have her, even if it's just long enough to get Evan back for what he did to me. I just want to tear that ass up. I'm not trying to get her hooked up in my and Evan's bullshit, but as a man, I have to handle my business. Christina Nelson meant everything to me. She was my world. Evan told her I had been cheating on her and that I was going to leave her for my new woman. A bitch ass move for a man to do just to get some ass. It worked because she left me before I even had the chance to tell her it was all a lie. April 20th, was the day she left. I got home from work, I opened my apartment door and as soon as I walked in I knew something was wrong. I yelled for Chris and I got no answer. I walked into my bedroom and the closet door was wide open. Half of the clothes that were inside when I left for work in the morning were gone. I checked the bathroom; everything of Chris' was gone. Everything that reminded me of her was gone. She even took the various pictures of us we had around the apartment. I hadn't noticed at first but she left a note for me on our bed. I picked up the note and read it:

Dear Sebastian,

I just wanted to let you know I'm so sorry I couldn't tell you I was leaving. I just couldn't face you. I've been seeing Evan for the past 2 months and I want to be with him. He told me you've been sleeping with someone else. How does it feel to have it done to you? If I'm wrong and Evan hasn't been completely honest with me then I'm sorry if I hurt you, but I still had to follow my heart and my heart is with Evan. One day I hope you forgive me for this.

-Chris

That's it, no other explanation. It completely crushed me. I sat on the floor in the middle of our room and lost it. I'm still not over it or over her. When I confronted Evan about it, he wasn't even man enough to admit to it. He denied everything that was in the letter. I tried to break his neck in his office, but two of his workers broke us up and I was escorted off of the property. I've done some dirt in my life, God knows I have, but I loved Chris, and I never cheated on her. I would have stayed with her for the rest of my life. Now it's like she has disappeared off the face of the earth. We were together for a year when all of this happened. Now I have the opportunity to get a little revenge and get my sexual fantasy girl. I couldn't believe it when I saw her at Studio 44. I saw her as soon as she walked in looking fine as hell and with her equally fine sister. I knew it was my time to get her the second she came out on the floor to dance with me.

Saniya's thickness is perfect. She has curves in all the right places. If this date goes as well as I want it to I will get her in somebody´s bed tonight. No matter what I have to do. Even if I have to drug that ass. I don't care how many porn movies she's been in, she aint never had no shit like this.

Here she is calling me now. "Hey pretty lady."

"Hey Sebastian, I'm running a few minutes late."

"It's cool, I kind of lost track of time too."

"I'll meet you there in about 15 minutes, is that ok?"

"Fine with me Saniya."

"Ok, see you then."

"Oh yeah, see you then."

Click. Yeah, tonight, that ass is mine!

The Sum of My Mistakes

Chapter Fourteen

Macy

Son of a bitch! He called the cops on me. Talking about I have a warrant for my arrest! "Let me out of this fucking police car!" I'm going to flip the fuck out if you don't let me out!"

"Mrs. Long, we will let you out as soon we get to the station and not a moment before, so please just calm down" the male officer said to me obviously very annoyed.

"Look, I haven't done anything wrong officers."

"Ma'am, we're just doing our job." The male officer tried to reason.

"I don't want to hear that bullshit!" I yelled back at the officer.

"Mrs. Long, please stop yelling and screaming at us, my partner and I are just doing our job, if you have done nothing wrong and this is all a misunderstanding, then there's nothing to worry about, then you'll be out very soon. If you continue to be a problem, we're going to have to add on disorderly conduct charges." This time it was the female officer who had spoken. I figured I better not press my luck, so I calmed down and began to think about how much money I owed for child support. $3,000 and some change. Maybe if I can bribe these officers, they will let me go. No, that won't work besides I have nothing to bribe them with. I have to figure out a way to get out of this. If they take me to the county they're going to take my finger prints. If there were any fingerprints left at that fire scene, I'm screwed.

"Officers may I make a phone call before we get to the station please." I tried the more gentle approach. The female officer spoke to me obviously tired of me and my mouth. "Mrs. Long, you will be able to make a phone call once they finish processing you, now that we've read you your rights and we're in transit to the County building, we're unable to allow you to make any phone calls."

"Well these handcuffs are uncomfortable can you at the very least loosen up the cuffs."

"Mrs. Long, we will adjust the cuffs as soon as we get to the county building." The female officer said. Shit! Nothing I say is working. I'd like to whip that female cop's ass talking to me like that! I'll get her name and badge number and get her ass later.

I decided I wasn't getting anywhere so I just sat there fuming. The female officer's phone rang. I had to listen to this bitch talking on the phone but they wouldn't allow me one three minute phone call. Her conversation seemed to go on forever. She's on the phone ooing and oow-ing sounding all stupid. Dumb bitch was pissing me off just from the sound of her voice. "Isn't it illegal for you guys to talk on your cell phones while you're driving people to jail?" I shouted from the back seat. Trying my best to interrupt her call. She turned around and stared at me for a few seconds. Then she began to whisper to her male partner. Dam she looks so familiar. I thought to myself. The whispering and that bullshit about not letting me make a phone call is really pissing me off now. Honestly, now that I think about it who am I going to call? Nobody will come and bail me out. I have no access to my money after Dayton cancelled all of our joint accounts and cancelled all of my credit cards. When I get done with his ass he'll wish he never got me arrested. I don't even know who's watching my daughter or I would go take her ass and hold her until he agrees to give me some damn money.

Now I kind of wish I didn't get Evan arrested, I know he would have given me a cash advance on my check and I could have paid some of the money and gotten out. Shit! Now I have no options. If only I could jump out of this damn car and make a run for it.

"I have to use the bathroom." I said trying to not be totally defeated. I really don't have to, but I'm trying to get them to pull over so I can run." "Mrs. Long, we will be there momentarily." The male officer spoke to me this time. That's when I realized there was nothing I could do but hope that everything burned in the fire. That fucking bitch Saniya was right; I didn't think all of this through. All I know now is I'm getting her ass, Dayton's ass and this bitch ass cop in passenger seat of this car. As soon as I get the hell out of here, which is God knows when.

We pulled into Union County Jail and the officer driving announced that we had arrived. "No shit" I replied back. The female officer got out of the passenger seat and walked to the door nearest to where I was sitting. She opened the door and told me to step out. "Mrs. Long, are those cuffs still bothering you?" She asked me but with a serious attitude.

"Yes, they are hurting like hell." I lied.

"Good." she whispered to me.

"Whatever." I said before I even had a chance to think about it. The female officer turned around and looked at me and began to laugh. She had a weird smile on her face and again I noticed she looked very familiar to me. "What are you fucking smiling at?" I spat at her.

"Nothing, nothing at all" She looked me right in my face and replied. "Mrs. Long I suggest you close your mouth, right the hell now before you accidently fall on your fucking face a few times" she whispered to me, her teeth clenched and fire in her eyes. Was that bitch trying to be funny? I thought to myself. I fucking hate females. Especially smart ass female cops. "Who in the fuck are you talking to?" I snapped at the female officer. Suddenly the male officer jumped and grabbed my handcuffs from the female officer. "It's cool, I got her" he said stepping in between us. The

female officer stood there for a few more seconds staring at me. What in

the hell is she looking at me like that for? I thought to myself, and

why does she look so damn familiar?

The male officer walked me through the doors leading to my new

temporary home. The female officer walked off and began to speak to

some other female officer. "What is your name officer?" I asked the male

officer.

"Officer Ronaldo Reyes he said obviously disgusted by my behavior and

relieved that he finally got me out of his car.

"And you're partner's name?

"Officer Wheeler, officer Jae'mi Wheeler."

Wheeler? No it can't be. I thought to myself. Then I yelled to the female

officer. "Hey... officer Wheeler, you got a sister named Saniya?"

The Sum of My Mistakes

Chapter Fifteen

Saniya

Dam I'm running late as hell for this date I have with Sebastian. I had to call Jae'mi and tell her the truth as to what was going on between Evan and I. Evan and I, wow that sounds so strange to me now. Here I am getting ready to go out on a date with another man. A friend of Evan's none the less. I know I shouldn't be doing this shit, but I'm leaving Evan as soon as I get him out of jail. I'm glad I spoke to Jae'mi about what was going on because now she's going to let me stay with her for a little while. The things that Evan has done to me in the past few months, I'd be a damn fool to stay with him. I can understand forgiving and forgetting, but that was the first 2 times. This time I'll just be being stupid if I take him back.

I know that stupid bitch Macy burned down the Plainfield store. I'm shocked she didn't burn down this house or his other property, or our Newark warehouse. Then she accuses him of sexual battery. That's deep. I wonder what the hell he said or did to her during their night together, to make her do all of these crazy things to him. Anyway, not really my business. If he hadn't been messing around on me in the first place, none of this stuff would be happening. If I had enough respect for myself to not take him back the first time he cheated, maybe all of this wouldn't have happened. I guess you live and you learn.

Now Sebastian. Mmm mm mm. Talk about sexy. As long as I worked out with Sebastian, I never really noticed how fine he was. I noticed he had a hell of a nice body, but I never looked at him like I did last night. He being Evan's friend should bother me but it doesn't. Besides, this isn't a hook-up; it's just dinner between two friends. I'm not really tempted by Sebastian. Besides, my head isn't quite right. After what I've just gone through with Evan, I'm not trying to get caught up with anybody. I don't think I'm ready for any type of relationship. Speaking of Sebastian, let me get my ass to Fridays, I know he's going to be looking for me.

Cool, I'm finally here... I think I see Sebastian's car. Let me call him and tell him I'm here. Ring... Ring... Ring..."Hello."

"Sebastian, hey it's Saniya, I'm here."

"Cool, I'm sitting in my car in the parking lot."

"Oh ok, I just pulled in."

"Oh, I see you. Come park on the other side of me, there's a free space."

"Cool, I'll be right there." I pulled my car around to the space on other side of Sebastian's car. I got out of my car as Sebastian got out of his. He had a bouquet of flowers in his hand." Damn he's looking good I thought to myself. "Hey Sebastian, good to see you again." I said to him as I approached him.

"Good to see you too beautiful, these are for you."

"Wow, thank you." I was so flattered. As I took the flowers from him. "Let's go on inside and grab something to eat." Sebastian said with so much enthusiasm it made me giddy. We walked into Fridays and all eyes were on us. There was a table full of women as soon as we walked in that stared us down. Sebastian must have noticed it too because he placed his hand around my waist and gave me a little squeeze. I felt proud to be with him. I smiled and waited for the hostess to seat us. Once we got to our seats Sebastian slid into the booth next to me instead of the seat across from me. Our server came over to our table immediately. We ordered our drinks and He and I talked the entire night. I told him about my situation with Evan and he told me about a few instances where he saw Evan out with other women. I was a bit annoyed with Sebastian for not coming to me and letting me know ahead of time and he explained to me that he just didn't want to be a part of Evan's bullshit. I understood exactly where he was coming from and he began to tell me the story of what happened between his girlfriend Chris and Evan. I can't believe Evan was messing with Sebastian's girlfriend. This is even more reason for me to get the hell away from him when he gets out of jail. I honestly have a good mind to not go and bail him out, but I'm going to at least do that. Then I'm going to sit him down and tell him I'm leaving him. I'm going to be a woman about it. Not going to just leave without an explanation. I guess things between us were worse than I thought they were.

Sebastian was saying everything a woman would love to hear. He made me feel beautiful and wanted. It was starting to get pretty late and I really needed to go home and go to bed. I had to get up early in the morning to go see about Evan. I needed to go to the bathroom so I asked Sebastian to order me one more drink, excused myself and off to the bathroom I went. I also checked my phone and realized I missed a call from my sister Jae'mi. I decided to call her back once I got home. I handled my business and washed my hands, and back to the table I went. When I got back to the table Sebastian had my drink waiting for me. I sat back down in the booth right next to Sebastian and took a few sips of my drink and that was the last thing I remembered clearly.

I woke up the next morning at first not knowing where the hell I was. Then I realized I was home and in my bed, completely naked and feeling like shit. I sat up and looked all over for my phone. It was nowhere to be found. "What in the hell happened last night?" I said out loud. I swung my legs around until they landed on the floor. I felt so sick to my stomach and sore all over. I went to stand up and was so weak I couldn't. I flopped back onto the bed and looked around the room for a second. I had to get my bearings. Finally I saw my purse sitting in the chair closest to my bed. I saw my cell phone hanging out of it and I could see the light flashing on it signaling I either had a text message or a voicemail. I knew I needed to get to my cell phone and call somebody to come and help me. I decided to slide off the bed and crawl to the chair to retrieve my purse and my phone. I slowly bent my knees and slid my bottom down the side of my bed until I landed on the floor. I placed my hands on the floor and pulled my body around and got on my belly. I began to pull myself towards the chair. When I finally reached the chair I felt like all of my energy was completely gone. My head was spinning and I felt like I had to throw up. I reached out for my purse and noticed that Officer Long's business card was sticking out of it. I checked my phone and saw that I missed six phone calls from Jae'mi, three phone calls from an unknown number and 1 call from Sebastian. I checked my voicemail and I had three messages from Evan. "Oh shit! I was supposed to meet with Officer Long this morning in regards to Evan's release. I looked at the wall clock in the room and it said 10:45 am. I was about to call Jae'mi back when my phone rang. It was Sebastian. "Hello."

"Hey beautiful, how are you feeling this morning?"

"Like shit Sebastian, what in the hell happened last night?" I snapped.

"Nothing much Saniya, you were pretty drunk, so I drove you home and put you in the bed." He didn't sound like he did yesterday. He sounded like he had something up his sleeve.

"Sebastian, did anything 'happen' between us last night?" I asked him, fearful of the answer.

"We made love Saniya." Sebastian said with nothing but happiness in his voice. I couldn't believe what he just said to me.

"What did you say?" I asked as I felt myself beginning to cry.

"We made love." Sebastian repeated.

"No!" I screamed into the phone. I was completely mortified at his words. "Sebastian, what do you mean we made love". I was so sick to my stomach I really thought I was going to throw up. I had never been so scared in my life. I can't for the life of me remember what the hell Sebastian felt like, I can't remember touching him, I can't remember anything. Just because I was scared didn't mean I wasn't going to use my head. I told Sebastian to hang on for a moment that I had another call. I placed him on mute and I found the voice record feature on my phone and hit it to record. I un-muted the phone and I continued my phone conversation with Sebastian making sure I had him to repeat everything he said and prayed his obviously unstable mind would say something to incriminate himself. "You put something in my drink Sebastian, What in the hell did you put in my drink?" I demanded.

"Just something to make you relax Saniya."

"You fucking drugged me!" I yelled into the phone. "Sebastian, ok I'm going to ask you how this "love making" started."

"Well Saniya, you came out of the bathroom you drank your last drink. Then, you told me you wanted to go home and make love. I brought you home and that's what we did, we made love in you and Evan's bed. He began to be very graphic and I realized I not only had I been violated but this asshole enjoyed what he did to me. I hung up the phone on Sebastian and picked up Officer Long's business card. I dialed the cell number that was written on the back. Ring...ring.....ring...."Officer D. Long speaking" I immediately broke down crying on the phone. "Officer Long, this is Saniya Wheeler, we met yesterday at the police station." "Yes of course Saniya, I remember you but what's wrong why are you crying?" " I think I've been raped!"

The Sum of My Mistakes

Chapter Sixteen

Sebastian

Oh shit, Saniya hung up on me. Let me try to call her back. Ring.... Ring... Ring... "Hi this is Saniya Wheeler; I'm unable to get to my phone right now. Please leave a message at the tone."

"Saniya its Sebastian, I think we got disconnected, please give me a call back, thanks." Shit! She didn't answer the phone. I know she's there, but she didn't answer. Those drugs I gave her should have worn off by now. I tried a few more times to call Saniya back, but she kept sending me to voicemail.

What a night I had with her last night. I fucked Saniya so good, it's a shame she was too high and out of it to remember. I took that beautiful body and entered her in every way I could. I licked and sucked and fucked her silly. What makes it even more special, it was in her and Evan's bed. The entire time I was there, I was wondering if Evan ever fucked Christina there. One thing does concern me though. I think I may have put a little too much of that GHB shit in Saniya's drink. She scared me for a minute slurring her speech and breathing all hard. Once she started breathing better and began to moan through our love making I fucked her and I left this morning before she woke up. Saniya knows she wanted me; She just needed a little bit of help expressing it to me. I can't wait to be inside of her again. I get hard just thinking about it. Glad I have this video I shot last night during our love making. Now I'll always have a way to remember my night with Saniya just in case it never happens again. The way I made her feel, she'll be back. Now I have to get my ass ready for work.

The Sum of My Mistakes

Chapter Seventeen

Dayton

"Saniya wait, calm down."

"Officer Long, I was raped!" Saniya yelled.

"I just need you to calm down enough to tell me what's going on." Even being a police officer, I couldn't believe what I was hearing. After speaking to Evan Roberts, Saniya's soon to be ex-boyfriend I found out that Saniya has had a few issues in her life, but she was doing an excellent job at getting her life together. No one deserves to be sexually assaulted. After I got Saniya calmed down a little, I began to understand what she was talking about. Apparently she went out on a date with her former personal trainer and he allegedly put something in her drink. She doesn't remember what happened after she accepted a drink from him, but woke up this morning in a lot of pain and very sick. I sent an ambulance and a police car to her home to get her to a hospital and start the process of taking her report. I promised her I would meet her at the hospital as soon as I could but I had to go check on Evan's potential release. I was able to talk with the judge and the prosecutor and get them to give Evan a bail. Hopefully he will be able to post bail and be released until his trial. I also had to inform Evan as to what was going on with Saniya and let him know she was in route to JFK hospital.

I got to the hospital and saw Saniya lying in the room and my heart sank. I had no idea why I had these feelings; I didn't even know this young lady I thought to myself. She was all alone and she looked like she was very scared. "Hello Saniya." I said trying not to sound like I felt sorry for her even though I did.

"Officer Long, thank you so much for coming and for sending the police and ambulance for me."

"You're welcome Saniya."

"They took my blood and I'm waiting for the dr. to come in and do a rape kit." Saniya said sounding very out of it. She said they gave her a sedative to calm her down. I felt the urge to hold her but decided not to act upon my urge. "Saniya can I get you anything or can I call anyone for you?"

"Could you please call my sister and let her know what's going on?"

"Of course I can do that for you, what's her name and number?" I asked as I pulled out my phone to dial.

"It's in my phone, over there, in my purse." I walked over to the table next to the bed where she was pointing and picked up Saniya's purse. I handed it to her and she found the number in her phone and handed the phone to me to call. "Her name is Jae'mi, Jae'mi Wheeler."

"Jae'mi Wheeler is your sister?" "Yes, do you know her?"

"I've seen her in passing many times over at the county courthouse."

"Yes, she's been a county officer for 3 years now."

"It's ringing... "Hello.""

"Hi Jae'mi Wheeler...this is Officer Long Plainfield Police Department, your sister Saniya Wheeler is here at JFK hospital and she needs for you to come to the hospital. She's ok but she needs for someone to come and be with her here in the hospital."

"Officer Long, what happened to her?" "I think you may want to let her explain that to you when you get here."

"Well, let her know I'm at work, I have to tell my supervisor what's going on and I'll be there as soon as I can."

"I will let her know and I'll stay here with her until you get here."

"Thank you Officer Long."

"You're very welcome Officer Wheeler."

"She'll be here soon, she's coming from work."

"Thank you Dayton." "You're welcome Saniya."

"Dayton, I hate to ask you, but can you stay with me until my sister gets here?" I know you might have things to do, and I understand if you can't."

"No, no I'm not going anywhere; I'm staying right here with you."

"Thank you so much she said." and then Saniya began to cry. I walked over to where she was and put my arms around her. "I'm so sorry this happened to you Saniya."

"I just can't believe he did this to me." Saniya whispered.

"It's ok, he's going to go to jail for this. I tried to reassure her.

"Dayton, thank you so much for staying with me."

"Yes Officer Long, thank you so much for helping my girl out." I heard his voice but was hoping it was my imagination.

"Evan." Saniya said looking just as surprised as I was..

"Mr. Roberts, good to see you." I said to Evan as I released Saniya."

"Thanks to you Officer Long, I'm out on bail."

"I'm glad you're out and I'm glad I could help." I said it, but now I wasn't sure if I meant it.

"Saniya baby, what happened?" Evan said filled with compassion and concern. Saniya once again began to cry. Evan and I switched places and he wrapped his arms around Saniya and held her. My heart sank again and suddenly I began to feel jealous, so I decided I needed to go.

"I'm going to go, if you guys need anything just give me a call."

"No Dayton, please stay." Saniya asked. Her eyes were pleading with me to stay.

"Yes Officer Long, please stay for a while." Evan said, not sounding sincere at all.

"Ok, I'll stay for a while. I'll be out in the lobby if you need me, I have to make a phone call and check on my daughter, I also needed to check on what was going on with my soon to be ex-wife. I didn't get a chance to tell you, she was arrested for nonpayment of child support. Thanks to Evan, I was able to get a good address on her and give it to the county officers. Hopefully the arson investigator will come up with some type of evidence while she's in there and she won't get out any time soon."

"Oh ok", Saniya said. She had actually calmed down, but she was obviously beginning to get upset all over again. She began to withdraw from Evan's arms and turn her back to him. I knew it was definitely time for me to make my exit.

I told them I'd be right back." With that said, I left the room and went to make my phone calls.

I made a few phone calls and was on the phone talking to my mom when I noticed Jae'mi walking into the automatic doors with panic all over her face. "Jae'mi" I called her name and she began to walk towards me. "Hi I'm Officer Dayton Long." I said to Jae'mi as I extended my hand to shake hers.

"I know I recognize you from the many times I've seen you at the county jail dropping off inmates. It's nice to finally meet you."

"You too." I replied. Jae'mi actually gave me a hug instead of shaking my hand.

"How's my sister?"

"They gave her a sedative, so she's a lot better than she was when she got here."

"So what exactly happened to her?"

"She was drugged and sexually assaulted by her former personal trainer."

"What? Really Sebastian?"

"Yes they apparently went out on a date and he put something in her drink, took her back to her own house and had sex with her and she doesn't remember any of it."

"Oh my God! She's been through so much the past few days."

"I know Evan told me, his version anyway."

"That bastard!"

"Yeah by the way, he's back there with her now."

"He's out of jail?"

"Yes he received a bail and bailed himself out."

"Wow! Well has that asshole Sebastian been arrested yet?"

"No, they are still gathering information, they are doing a rape kit on her soon and they took her blood so far." Right then Evan came walking down the hallway. "Evan, is everything ok?" I asked.

"Yes, they are doing the rape kit on her now."

"Oh ok." Good after those results we should be able to get the warrant for Sebastian's arrest.

"Hello Jae'mi." Evan directed his attention to her.

"Evan, don't say shit to me, if it wasn't for you she wouldn't be going through this bullshit!"

"I know Jae'mi and I'm really so sorry about all of this." Evan said. He actually sounded quite sincere.

"Save it Evan." Jae'mi snapped. Evan backed off and walked away.

"Thank you for all of your help Officer Long." Jae'mi said to me.

"Anytime Officer Wheeler and stop calling me officer, just call me Dayton." Jae'mi chuckled a little and agreed as long as I called her Jae'mi. I had a feeling she and I would see more of each other through Saniya. I had already decided I was going to be a part of Saniya's life in any way I could.

Jae'mi and I sat down in the lobby of the hospital waiting for one of the nurses to come and get us for us to go back in the room with Saniya. Evan decided to try and talk to Jae'mi despite her obvious disgust with him. Jae'mi decided to not act ugly with him here at the hospital. They walked outside to talk and the nurse came out to inform us that we could go back into the room with Saniya. She wanted us to only go one person at a time, so I decided to go back first and check on her while Evan and Jae'mi were outside talking. I entered the room and Saniya looked at me and her face lit up. "May I come in?" I asked.

"Oh please do" she replied. She was actually smiling a little. I walked over to Saniya and again I got that weird feeling in my stomach. I sat down in the chair next to her bed. I was about to ask her what the doctor said when the investigating officers tapped on the door and we both turned around and said "Come in." Although they and Saniya agreed I could stay during the questioning, I figured I would step out and let Jae'mi and Evan know we were able to see her again. As I went to walk outside, Jae'mi was telling Evan to go fuck himself, and he was once again walking away. I walked up to Jae'mi and told her we could go see Saniya again as soon as the officers were done. Jae'mi was so frustrated; she didn't even hear me at first. "Jea'mi, we can go back in the room and see her as soon as the investigating officers are done."

"Thanks Dayton." She said quickly.

"What's going on with Evan?" I cautiously asked Jae'mi

"He said he needs to go to the fire department and get some report and call up the insurance company and check on his claim."

"Now?" I said in surprise.

"Yep, he thinks that's more important than Saniya right now." Jae'mi said sounding quite annoyed and disappointed.

"Wow, that's deep." I replied completely taken aback by Evan's obvious selfish behavior. I'm glad I consider myself a real man. I could never let the person I love to go through something like this alone. I kept my opinion to myself and volunteered to stay with Saniya as long as she was going to be here. I felt a deep connection with her and if my feelings were

116

right, she felt a connection with me too. "Here come the officers doing Saniya's case." I told Jae'mi.

"Dayton." Officer Clemente called out to me."

"What's up?" I responded. I walked over to my two fellow officers, hoping they had some good news for me." "She was definitely raped, according to the doctor." Officer Robin Clemente said with a very serious look on her face. Her partner Officer Reggie Erickson informed me they were going back to headquarters to work on the warrant for Sebastian's arrest. I introduced Jae'mi to both officers, and they also remembered her from the county building. We all chatted for a while and I realized Saniya was all alone in her room. So Jae'mi and I said our goodbyes and the officers left. I couldn't wait to get back to that room and make sure Saniya was ok.

Hours had gone by and Jae'mi, Saniya and I had all fallen asleep. Evan did at least call a few times to check on Saniya so he can't be too bad of a guy. Macy was unable to come up with the child support money to bail herself out and she hadn't seen a judge as of yet so she was still in jail. My daughter was safe and sound with my parents and Saniya was safe and sound with me. I decided to take a personal day today just in case Saniya and Jae'mi needed me to be there when they released Saniya. I don't know if they need me, but I just wanted to be there just in case. It was six in the morning when I woke up and saw that I had a few missed calls and I had three voice mails. I dialed my voice mail and got the message that they arrested Sebastian. I was so happy. I don't know what has me so involved in Saniya and her life, but I felt something for her. Something I can't explain right now. I noticed Saniya was waking up and I walked over to say good morning to her.

"Good morning Saniya."

"Good morning Dayton, you stayed here all night?"

"Yes I did, I didn't want you and Jae'mi to be alone."

"Thanks Dayton, where's your little girl?"

"She's with my parents."

"Oh ok good."

"My little girl is with her father. Hopefully I can go home today and see her, I miss her so much and I didn't want her to see me in the hospital and looking like this."

"Oh I understand that." I said.

"Good morning people" Jae'mi said finally waking up.

"Good morning" Saniya and I said in unison. We looked at each other and laughed.

"Well now that both of you are up I have some great news." I began to speak to the girls. "Sebastian has been arrested."

"Oh yes!" Saniya said happy as hell. It was the first time since she got to the hospital I saw her smile. She has a beautiful smile, I thought to myself.

The doctor came in and they released Saniya. I found out that she was moving in with Jae'mi and not going back home to Evan. For some reason I felt relieved. I decided to go home, change my clothes, go check on my little one and stop over at Jae'mi's house later to check up on Saniya. I felt so empty when I realized I was leaving Saniya. I walked them to Jae'mi's car and off they drove off. I was walking to my car when out of nowhere Evan approached me. "Officer Long, may I speak to you for a minute."

The Sum of My Mistakes

Chapter Eighteen

Evan

Officer Dayton Long is becoming a bit of a problem. He's been hanging around Saniya since I got arrested. I walk into her hospital room and he has his arms wrapped around her. I know Saniya is going through some rough shit right now, but if she hadn't been calling herself going on a date with another man, this shit wouldn't have happened. When I get my hands on Sebastian I'm going to fuck him up. How dare he have sex with my woman! If I could kill his ass and get away with it I would.

Saniya telling me she doesn't want to be with me anymore, that's bullshit. I know I fucked up and I made a lot of mistakes, but all I'm asking for from her is to give me another chance. I don't think that's unreasonable. Hopefully these charges against me will be dropped and I can rebuild the Plainfield store and move on with my life. Jae'mi hanging around Saniya isn't going to work either. She doesn't understand our relationship so of course she's going to tell Saniya not to fuck with me anymore. Of course Saniya's going to listen to her sister.

Now here I am sitting here in my damn car waiting for Saniya and Jae'mi to pull off so I can have a little conversation with Officer Long. Finally they pulled off. I got out of my car and walked up behind Officer Long, obviously I caught him off guard. "Officer Long, May I speak to you for a minute?"

"Of course Evan, you want to talk here or go somewhere else? He asked.

"I think somewhere else may be better." I said as I continued to approach him.

"Ok Evan let me get my car and you can follow me."

"Sure, ok let me get my car too I said." He'd actually caught me a little off guard. I decided to go ahead and follow him, so I got my car and pulled up behind him. He hung a left and went to the end of the block. We made a right at the first light and then traveled down the road until we hit the next light. We hung a left and drove down the road a little way until we reached Edison Diner. He pulled in the parking lot, and parked, I parked right next to him. We both got out of our cars and headed for the door. He politely held the door for me as we entered the diner. We took a booth and sat down. The waitress came over to us and asked if we'd like something to drink. We both ordered coffee and I decided to get something to eat. We ordered breakfast and when the waitress walked away I began to speak.

"Officer Long, I just want to say I really appreciate all that you have done for me and for Saniya these past few days."

"Evan please stop calling me Officer Long, and call me Dayton, and you're both very welcome. So what do you want to talk to me about?" he asked.

"Dayton, I'll get straight to the point. I think you have a thing for Saniya and she's my lady and I don't plan on letting her go." I said with a stern tone in my voice.

"Wow Evan." Dayton said with a bit of sarcasm in his voice. "Where did that come from?"

"It came from me seeing you with your arms around her yesterday and you staying in her room all night last night."

"Evan, I don't normally feel the need to explain myself to anyone, but since you seem a little insecure about my new friendship with Saniya, I'll ease your mind a little bit. I had my arms around her because she had just been through a traumatic experience; she was crying and needed someone to hold her. There was no one else there but me. Now if you had been there for your lady I wouldn't have had to. As far as me being there for her all of last night, Jae'mi asked me to stay there just in case you showed back up because you were not very pleasant to her when you were there earlier. Now if you had come back to be with your lady and had been a little more pleasant to her sister, again I wouldn't have had to." At that moment I realized I looked like a complete fool. I'm so busy stating my claim and trying to hold on to Saniya, I made myself look insecure and petty.

"I wasn't trying to offend you Dayton, I just want you to back off a little and let me gain Saniya's trust again."

"Look Evan, I don't know what's going on between the two of you, but this isn't the way to gain her trust back."

"Man I don't know what to do; I really fucked up with her."

"Pray about it man, but approaching me and trying to flex your muscles won't work. You watched her pull off from the hospital and instead of talking to her and making sure she was ok, you let her pull off and decided reprimanding me was more important than she is."

"You're right man." I said obviously defeated. I had just fucked this man's wife 2 days before and he did nothing but help me and Saniya in our time of need. I need to check myself but not in front of Dayton.

Dayton's phone rang and he got up and walked away to take the call. I decided to give Saniya a call and check on her. Immediately her phone went to voicemail. I wondered if that was her calling Dayton. He returned back to our table and said he had to make our conversation short. "I have to run and check on my daughter." He said as he signaled for the waitress to come to the table.

"Look Dayton, I'm not trying to seem unappreciative for what you did for me, I'm just trying to protect my lady." I said hoping this would smooth over whatever bad feelings he may have developed for me.

"No hard feelings Evan. Just remember, Macy had a husband and you did whatever you did with her." I immediately began to think about What happened between Macy and me and once again I felt embarrassed.

"I'm sorry man, Macy never told me about you."

"And I'm sure you never asked her either."

"No man I didn't." I said completely embarrassed by this time. This little meeting definitely didn't go as planned. Only thing I managed to do was embarrass myself. Dayton got his food to go, paid our bill, shook my hand and said goodbye. I decided to sit there in that booth for a while and think about my life and some of the things I have been doing. Shit just doesn't seem to be working for me at all.

I was scared to go home and face Saniya. I had done absolutely nothing to protect her. I've done nothing but hurt her for no reason. Maybe the best thing I can do for her is to let her leave.

I got into my car to leave Edison Diner and my phone began to ring.... I looked at the number and didn't recognize it. I answered it anyway.

"Hello."

"Evan, its Macy, please don't hang up!"

"Bitch, don't you ever call me ever again!" I yelled into the phone.

CLICK! I hung up on Macy's ass.

Macy continued to call my phone over and over again. I kept sending her to voicemail. No way in hell I was going to talk to that bitch! I drove around Plainfield and Edison for a while thinking about what I would say to Saniya when I got home. It's been two hours and I still haven't been able to go home and face her. Macy called my phone at least a dozen and half times in the two hours I drove around. I made a mental note to stop by Plainfield Police Department and file harassment charges against Macy. I also decided to call my lawyer and let her know what was going on with Macy's calls. Then I decided to go to Plainfield Fire Department and check to see if they had a copy of my fire report ready. I needed it for the Insurance company. I was just trying to keep busy until I actually had to go home and face Saniya.

After running my errands for most of the day, I finally got home and Saniya's car isn't in the garage. My heart sank. I knew what I was walking into. I opened the garage door leading into the house. I felt the emptiness as soon as I walked into the house. I walked into the kitchen and opened the fridge. I pulled out a bottle of wine and got a glass out of the cabinet. I walked into Azera's room first and confirmed what I was feeling in my heart. Most of her clothes and toys were gone. I walked out of her room and into my bedroom and saw the bed where Sebastian raped Saniya. Our bed. I stood there for a second and the tears began to fall. I knew she was gone. I fell to my knees and lost it. I cried uncontrollably for what seemed like hours.

After that downpour of emotion. I finally stood up and walked over to Saniya's closet. I opened it up and most of her clothes were gone. I grabbed one of the dresses she left behind and walked over to Saniya's dresser. I pulled out the top drawer...empty. I took the dress, the wine and the glass I was carrying back downstairs this time to the living room. I sat down on the couch and poured myself a glass of wine. I looked up on our mantel at the picture of Saniya and me. That's where I noticed an envelope with my name on it taped to the mantel. I got up from the couch, grabbed the envelope and sat back on the couch. I opened the envelope and found

Saniya's house key and a short letter from her. This is what it read:

Dear Evan,

I waited for you to come home while I grabbed a few of my things, but after 2 hours you never showed. I didn't want to do this without saying goodbye to you, but you left me no choice. I hope everything works out for you. I'm no longer able to be in a relationship with you for obvious reasons. There are far too many chances that have been given. I'm tired Evan. I'm Just so very tired. I'll call you when I'm ready to come back and get the rest of my things. Take care of yourself.

-Saniya

That was it. No I hate you or go to hell. No question as to why I did what I did to her. Just simply goodbye. I downed the first glass of wine and poured myself another glass. I downed that one too and poured myself another one. I was determined to drown my pain tonight. I didn't think if she left that it would hurt this much, I thought to myself. Part of me wanted to call her and beg her to come back, but that was just the selfish side of me. Saniya deserves better and I know that. I've always known that. I want to be the one to give her better, I just don't know how.

I decided I would try to give Saniya a call to see if she would talk to me. I had no idea what I would say, but I tried it anyway. I dialed her number and it began to ring. Like I thought she would, she sent me to voicemail. I left a message. "Saniya, this is Evan. I just wanted to call and check on you. Please give me a call back when you get my message. Thanks. Click. I continued to call her number and leave messages for 3 more hours. Still she wouldn't answer the phone. I knew she was more than likely staying at Jae'mi's house. I drank so much I got an S on my chest and decided to try and go over to Jae'mi's house to talk to Saniya. I attempted to stand up from the couch and fell forward onto the floor I was so intoxicated. I decided it was best that I stay my drunk ass home so I grabbed a pillow off of the couch and propped it under my head on the floor. There is where I stayed until my phone went off and woke me up the next day. Ring...Ring....Ring..... I found my phone and answered it. That's when I received horrible news. My ex-wife Asia was in a horrible car accident and wasn't expected to live. My kids have no one but me now. I jumped up off the floor and headed to the door to go to the hospital. I opened my door and Macy was standing there on my steps about to ring my doorbell. What in the fuck?

The Sum of My Mistakes

Chapter Nineteen

Saniya

Whew! Finally I'm settled. It was a lot moving all that stuff out in 2 hours. We finally got most of our things moved into Jae'mi's house. Thank God Dayton met us here to help us unload. He's been such a great new friend. He's been here every minute I've needed him and I'm definitely not used to that.

Jae'mi is so much more than a sister, she's my rock.

Azera finally got "home". I didn't want her to see me this out of it, so I'm trying to be strong so she doesn't worry. She wants to know why we have to move in with Auntie Jae'mi, I'm going to try and explain it all to her tonight.

Dayton ran out to get us all something to eat. I still wonder why he's being so nice to us. He doesn't even know us. I must admit when he held me last night it felt so good. No one has ever held me like that. My sister keeps referring to him as my new boyfriend. I'm trying to laugh it off but truth be told, I can't handle any type of relationship right now. After what Evan did and now after what Sebastian did to me, I can't trust anyone enough to get close to anyone right now. Speaking of Evan, he has been calling me like crazy all day and all night. I don't have the energy for Evan. I'm all used up. I know he wants to try and talk me out of leaving him but I'm not falling for it.

"Saniya, the food is here." Jae'mi called from the living room.

"I'm coming!" I yelled back.

I got up from the bed and made my way to the stairs and smelled the Jamaican food. All of a sudden I didn't want the food anymore. I felt sick to my stomach and I just wanted to lie back down. I swallowed hard and decided to suck it up and go get myself something to eat. Once I got downstairs I felt a little better. I straightened out my face and walked into the kitchen and saw Dayton handing a plate of food to Azera. I had to let out a little smile. He was so gentle with her and so kind.

I looked at the table and saw all of the food Dayton had gotten for us. All of my favorites. Oxtails, curry chicken, baked red snapper, peas and rice, macaroni pie, fried plantains, cabbage and vegetables. "Wow Dayton, these are all of my favorites." I said finally able to really smile. I tried not to let the nausea I felt show on my face.

"I didn't know what you liked, so I got a little bit of everything."

"Thank you, I can't wait to make my plate, hurry up Jae'mi and move out of my way, I'm hungry." I said, realizing I hadn't eaten in 2 days. I made my plate and then went into the dining room and took a seat across from Dayton. I was really enjoying my dinner and happy I had my sister and Dayton here to protect me. I felt so safe with them being around. I didn't know how I would make ends meet and I know I have a rough road ahead of me when it comes to the charges I filed against Sebastian, but at this moment I feel like everything would be ok as long as I don't let myself get too down about all the things that have happened to me lately. I have to stay strong and stick to my guns no matter how hard things get. With my past I know a trial wouldn't be that easy, but no matter what I have to do I will make sure I stick to my guns and not let Sebastian get away with what he did to me. "Saniya, are you done with your plate?" Jae'mi was talking to me but I guess I had drifted off into my own world.

"Oh, I'm sorry Jae'mi, no I'm going to get a little more food, I'm still a little hungry."

Dayton finished his plate and walked into the kitchen to throw the empty plate away. "Saniya, I'm going to head on home, I really need to see my little girl." he said.

"Oh, ok. Dayton, thank you so much for everything you've done for me."

"You're welcome Saniya and you said that like you're never going to see me again. I'll be by to check on you tomorrow." he said smiling that big pretty smile he had at the police station the first day I met him. I'll be honest; I was so relieved when Dayton said he'll be back. I just assumed he had had enough of me and all of my issues and I wouldn't see him for a little while at least.

"No, it's not like that Dayton; I guess I'm just a little emotional."

"Oh I understand that Saniya after all you've been through the last few days."

"Yeah, I guess you're right."

"Try to go upstairs and get some rest and if you can't sleep and you feel like talking, give me a call."

"Thanks Dayton, but I know I've taken up far too much of your time already, I'm a big girl I'll be ok." Truth was I was scared to death to go to sleep tonight. The hospital had given me a prescription for some sleeping pills, so I had those to get me to sleep, but with everything on my mind, I knew there was no way I would be able to stay sleep all night. Dayton turned around to head to the living room to say goodbye to Jae'mi and Azera. "Goodbye ladies, I'll be back to check on all of you tomorrow, if that's ok with you Jae'mi."

"Dayton, you're welcome to my house anytime, thank you for everything you've done for my sister."

"Like I told her, you're very welcome, and if you ladies need me before I get by here tomorrow, just give me a call. Jae'mi, you have my number right?"

"Yes I do!"

"Ok cool." Dayton said as he headed to the door. I can't believe this, but I don't want to see him go. I thought to myself but I kept my cool and my feelings to myself and walked Dayton to the door. He turned to me and said "Goodnight Saniya."

"Good night Dayton." with that, he left.

Immediately after Dayton left my cell phone started to ring. I sent Azera upstairs to get my phone. She came down the stairs talking to somebody on the phone. She got to the bottom of the steps and handed me the phone. I looked down and Evan's name was on the screen. Azera had answered the phone not realizing that I didn't want to speak to Evan. Instead of hanging up like I wanted to, I put the phone to my ear and said "Hello" I said with no enthusiasm in my voice.

"Hi Saniya."

"Yes Evan."

"How are you Saniya?"

"I'm ok." I said again with no enthusiasm.

"I was just calling to check on you and to tell you that Asia was in a terrible car accident and she probably won't survive."

"Oh Evan, I'm so sorry to hear that, where are the kids?" I asked thinking about them and what they must be going through.

"I'm with them now, here at the hospital."

"Oh my God, please tell them I said hello and if they need anything to give me a call."

"Ok, I will, I'm going to be taking them to the house, I was wondering if there was any way you could come by and see them."

"Evan, that's not going to happen."

"Oh ok, I understand Saniya, I just wanted to ask."

"Ok well, Evan I have to go."

"Ok Saniya."

"Goodbye Evan."

Click. I pressed 'end call' on my phone before he could say anything else. I finally got Azera to sleep and began to feel tired myself. I pulled out the sleeping pills the hospital gave me. I shook the bottle and thought about what it would be like if I wasn't here anymore. I could take this entire bottle of pills and end it all I thought. No, I could never do that I reasoned. I could never leave my baby girl here alone. I know Jae'mi would take care of Azera but there's nothing like a mother's love. Having Azera saved me from myself and I could never betray her like that. I stopped thinking all crazy and got up to go to the kitchen and get myself some juice to take my pill. I checked my cell phone and I had three text messages, two from Evan and one from Dayton. Evan's text messages were him saying he's so sorry for everything he did and keeping me updated on what was going on with Asia. Dayton wanted to say good night, but didn't want to take the chance of calling and waking me up. That message was left just two minutes before I checked them. I put the sleeping pill in my mouth and took a quick drink of juice and swallowed it down. I lay down in the bed next to Azera. I picked up my phone and dialed Dayton's number. He answered on the first ring. "Hi Saniya"

"Hi Dayton, I got your text. I figured I would call and say good night."

"I'm glad you called Saniya I was just thinking about you." I was blushing a little when Dayton said that. I could hear his little girl cooing and laughing in the background."Ooo I hear the baby, she sounds wide awake", I said to change the subject. Dayton laughed and said "yep, she's up and ready to play and I'm tired and I want to go to bed"

"Aww Dayton, through all of the madness I never had a chance to ask you your daughter's name."

"Oh yes you're right. It's Serenity, Serenity Dawn Long."

"Wow, that's a beautiful name Dayton."

"Thank you Saniya, It really fits her little personality. She's definitely my peace and serenity. I hope when she gets older she likes it." Dayton said.

"I'm sure she will." I tried to re-assure him

I responded trying to reassure him. I suddenly began to feel a little dizzy and very tired. I guessed the sleeping pill I took was kicking in. "Dayton, I took a sleeping pill and I'm so sorry I'm beginning to feel very sleepy."

"Ok Saniya, are you in the bed?"

"Yes," I said drifting off.

"Ok, then, good night Saniya, I'll see you tomorrow."

"Good night Dayton." I said then I drifted off to sleep, but I wouldn't stay sleep for long.

I was having thoughts about what happened with Sebastian. I kept dreaming that he was forcing me to have sex with him. I was lying on the bed and he was taking my clothes off. I tried to fight him off but I was too weak to do so. He spread my legs and slid himself into me. I was screaming for him to let me go but he wouldn't. I was naked and in the middle of a field right out in the open. There were people cheering him on and the louder the crowd cheered the more forceful he got. I just kept screaming to get him off of me but nobody would help me. I must have been screaming for real because Azera was crying for me to wake up and Jae'mi came running in the room. I busted out into tears and Jae'mi threw her arms around me and held me. After I calmed down a bit, I looked over at the clock on the nightstand and it was 4 o'clock in the morning. After I apologized to Jae'mi and Azera for waking them up, I sent both of them back to bed and I went downstairs and climbed onto the couch to watch some TV. I was so tired and sleepy. I thought about Dayton and wondered if he was awake. I decided to take my chance and see if he was up. I was so scared to go back to sleep. Dayton has been such a great new friend. I don't want to push my luck with him, but to be honest I didn't have anyone else to talk to. I dialed Dayton's number and he answered on the first ring. "Hey you" Dayton said as he answered the phone. I immediately started crying as soon as I heard his voice. "Saniya, what's wrong?" He asked.

"Dayton I had a horrible dream and I can't sleep!" I cried. I couldn't believe I was being so vulnerable with Dayton.

"I'll be right over Saniya."

"Dayton, it's 4 in the morning and I know you have your little girl."

"I've been at my parent's house for the past few weeks, my mom gets up at this time every day, she'll watch Serenity for me and I'll be right there."

"Okay" I said too emotionally drained to argue the point. Dayton and I hung up and 20 minutes later he was back at Jae'mi's house, saving me from my horrible dream. He came in the house and never said anything but "Hey." Tears were streaming down my face and he just wiped them away. He sat down on the couch and placed a pillow on his lap. He grabbed my hand and pulled me down on the couch next to him. He patted the pillow so I could lay my head down. I lay down and rolled onto my left side so that my face would be facing Dayton's body. He once again wiped away the tears from my eyes, and moved hair away from my face. Suddenly I felt so relaxed and safe. I closed my eyes and began to drift off to sleep. Next thing I knew I was waking up to the sound of Azera whispering to me. "Mommy...get up." she said. I opened my eyes and saw that Dayton was gone. Part of me felt a little sad, but I was so happy he came over this morning and put me back to sleep. I asked Jae'mi what time it was and she said it was noon. I jumped up to get Azera something to eat, but Jae'mi said she already fed her breakfast and lunch. My sister is the best.

Jae'mi said that Dayton left around 8 in the morning saying he had to go get his baby girl but he said he would be back a little later. I felt so much better that I got some sleep. I got up, got myself some coffee and a bagel and cream cheese to eat.

While I was eating, I decided to do Jae'mi a favor and cook Sunday dinner for everyone. I'm a wonderful cook. I decided to go to the grocery store and pick up all of the items I needed to make dinner. I jumped up from the couch and walked into the kitchen to talk to my sister. "Hey Jae'mi, I'm going to cook dinner for everyone tonight."

"Cool, what are you going to cook?" She asked seeming very excited.

"What would you like?" I asked her.

"Hmmm." Some seafood would be nice or some fried chicken, fried cabbage, macaroni and cheese and peach cobbler." She fired at me.

"Mmm, that sounds perfect Jae'mi." I decided to go take a shower and get dressed to go to the store. Ring... Ring... Ring...my phone started ringing. I didn't recognize the number that came up. So I sent the call to voicemail. Two minutes later my phone rang again. Again, I didn't recognize the number. I again sent it to voicemail. I attempted to get into the shower and my phone rang again. I answered it with nothing but attitude in my voice "Hello!" I yelled into the phone.

"Saniya, don't hang up, it's me Sebastian."

"You fucking bastard, how dare you fucking call me after what you did to me!" I yelled so loud Jae'mi heard me and came running up the stairs to see what was wrong. I hung up the phone and threw it across the room. Thank God it landed on the bed and didn't break. "What happened Saniya? Who was that?" Jae'mi asked.

"That was Sebastian's ass; he had the nerve to call me." I said now completely in tears again. Jae'mi walked over the bed and picked up my phone.

"That means he violated his restraining order and you need to call the police department and file a report. After we're done doing that, we need to go to contact T-Mobile and change your cell phone number." She reasoned.

"What if Dayton tries to call me?" I said finally trying to calm myself down.

"We'll call him now and tell him what's going on. I'm sure he can send someone over here to take the violation of the restraining order report for you."

I was so glad I had Jae'mi for a sister. She was smart as hell and her being a corrections officer came in really handy." I dialed Dayton's number and he picked up right after the first ring. "Hey Saniya, what's up?"

"Hey Dayton, Sebastian just called me."

"What?! He just called you?"

"Yes, he did." I cried.

"What did you say to him when he called?" Dayton asked

"Nothing, I hung up as soon as I heard his voice."

"Well, I'm not sure if he was ever officially served with the restraining order Saniya."

"Oh ok, so what should I do now?"

"I'll call up headquarters and find out if he was ever served. Then I'll send over an officer to take the report that he violated if he did. I would come over, but my mom's not here to look after Serenity."

"Do you mind bringing her with you?" I said feeling like I needed him here with me.

"No, I don't mind bringing her at all; I'll pack her bag and be right there."

"Ok, and again thank you Dayton."

"Stop thanking me, I'm doing things for you because I want to Saniya."

"Ok I'm sorry; I'll try to stop saying thank you so much."

"It's ok, that means your mama raised you right." Dayton said joking with me. I actually laughed a little. It was the first time in a few days that I actually laughed. I hung up the phone and sat down next to Jae'mi on the bed. "Is it ok if Dayton brings the baby over Jae'mi?" I was so upset about Sebastian calling me that I forgot to ask my sister if it was ok for the baby to be here.

"Of course Saniya, I would love to meet Dayton's little one." Once again, I thought to myself, I have such a wonderful sister. My phone rang again, and the same number popped up. This time, Jae'mi answered the phone. "Hello." She said with authority in her voice. "Sebastian stop calling Saniya's phone she doesn't want to talk to you." She said it in a nice calm but authoritative manner. Sebastian must have finally got the message and hung up on Jae'mi. Hopefully he got the hint.

Dayton got to the house an hour after we spoke on the phone. I was all showered and refreshed and in a far better mood than I was when we spoke on the phone. Evan called my phone four times since 11:00 am, and he was calling again. He left a message but I never bothered checking my voicemail. The only people I wanted to be bothered with were right here in the house. When Dayton walked into the front door he looked and smelled so good. He had Serenity sitting in her little car seat and had her diaper bag hanging from his shoulder. I'll admit I was feeling a little weird about seeing Macy's daughter. After the hell that woman caused me, I shouldn't have wanted to have anything to do with her soon-to-be ex-husband or her daughter, but Dayton was too nice of a guy for me to not get to know him and his daughter a little better. He walked in and immediately placed Serenity and her car seat on the couch. Her face was covered with her baby blanket. I didn't want to seem too anxious but I wanted to see what she looked like. Dayton put down the diaper bag and took the blanket from over her face. I saw her little face. She was absolutely adorable. She looked exactly like Dayton. His nose, the shape of his face and his thick beautiful lips. I wasn't able to see what her eyes looked like, because she was sleeping, but she had long beautiful eyelashes. He tried to take off her little sweater but you could tell he couldn't quite get it off. I walked over to them and picked her up out of the seat to get the sweater off of her. Why he had a sweater on her in the first place as warm as it was, I have no idea. But as a new daddy I know he didn't know any better. As I pulled her arms out of her sweater she began to wake up. Then I saw those big beautiful eyes and I was hooked. I fell in love with her instantly. It didn't matter who her mother was, I was now in love with this adorable little girl.

She began to cry and Dayton reached into her bag to get her a bottle.

"When was the last time she ate Dayton?" I asked him placing her on my chest.

"She just finished a bottle." He answered looking a little tired. I propped her up on my left shoulder and she instantly stopped crying. She put her little fingers in her mouth and began to suck on them. "Dayton, she's teething, that's why she's so uncomfortable." I told him. He looked so relieved.

"Saniya, I thought I was doing something wrong."

"No not at all, she just needs a teething ring and some baby Orajel."

"Oh ok, should I go get it now?"

"Ha ha, yes Dayton, run up to Walgreens and pick up some baby Orajel and a couple of teething rings."

"Ok." He said looking quite relieved. My big knight in shining armor looked so confused.. Jae'mi walked up behind me and began to play with the baby. "Saniya, why don't you go to the store with Dayton and help him find what he needs, I'll keep little Serenity and Azera here with me. Then you can get the stuff for dinner too."

"Are you sure Jae'mi?"

"Positive sis." "Ok, let me get my purse, come on Dayton."

"Yes ma'am" he said joking with me.

Dayton and I jumped into his truck and headed to Walgreens. "So, you're cooking dinner tonight Saniya." He said.

"Yes I am Officer Long." I replied.

"Umm, can you cook? I'm just asking." Dayton said joking with me.

"Yeah, I can cook!" I said joking back with him." I felt so comfortable with Dayton and I enjoyed his sense of humor.

"We'll see Ms. Saniya Wheeler."

"Yes we will Officer Dayton Long." We both laughed. Dayton was so handsome in his white tee-shirt, dark blue cargo shorts and sandals. He had a nice tattoo that said Serenity on his right bicep and a dark blue fitted baseball cap on. I was able to see his thick arms and sexy legs.

We arrived at Walgreens and immediately I noticed that Evan's car was in the parking lot. I told Dayton to just keep driving to Shoprite instead. We could have gotten the food and come back to Walgreens after Evan left, but instead Dayton completely ignored me and pulled into the Walgreens parking lot. He pulled into the lot and parked the SUV. He turned the truck off, placed his hand on mine and said follow my lead. Dayton pulled the door handle and got out of the car. He walked around to my side of the car and opened my door, grabbed my hand and guided me out of the car. I got out and looked around to see if I could see Evan anywhere. Walgreens on a Sunday is packed. I didn't see any signs of Evan in the parking lot. We walked into the automatic doors and I immediately saw Evan out the corner of my eye, standing in line. Dayton grabbed my hand and walked me straight up to Evan. "What's up man, how are you?" Dayton said to Evan smiling.

"Hi Saniya" Evan said then he put his head down and stared at the floor. He looked so hurt. Then I heard the kids calling my name.

"Miss Saniya!" Little Evan said grabbing me around my waist and hugging me.

"Evan, Isis! How are you guys?" I said with tears forming in my eyes. I missed the kids so much and I was so glad to see them"

"Hello Saniya." I heard her voice, but I couldn't believe it.

"Macy!" Dayton said with fury in his voice. Macy walked up right next to Evan and stood there. I couldn't believe my eyes.

"Go to hell Macy." I said to her and then I turned around and I started to walk away. Evan walked up behind me calling my name.

"Saniya, please listen to me, it's not what it seems."

"Evan I don't care what it is."

I hadn't noticed it at first, but Macy was walking right behind us. Suddenly

146

she began calling my name and calling me an arsonist. I started walking more quickly to get away from both Evan and crazy ass Macy. Then Evan yelled down the aisle "Saniya, I know you burned down my store and I'm pressing charges against you." I stopped right in my tracks.

"Evan, you know damn well I didn't burn down that store!" I yelled back at him.

"Prove it in court!" He snapped.

"Who put that in your head Evan, Macy?" Dayton said that remark obviously pissed him off.

"Mind your business Officer Long." Evan said, snapping at Dayton. "Man, you're lucky I'm a cop! You're gonna try and talk shit to me when I got you out of trouble when Macy got your ass locked up on trumped up charges, now you're hanging with her ass? What the hell is wrong with you man? Think Evan! Don't let her manipulate you man, and ruin Saniya's life."

"Mind, your fucking business Dayton, Macy is dropping those charges against me and she apologized to me for filing them!" I couldn't believe what I was hearing. Evan's ass was siding with Macy. He really thought I burned down that store. I had had enough of Macy's bullshit. "Come on Saniya, let's get the stuff we need for Serenity and get the hell out of here."

Dayton finally said grabbing my hand and pulling me away from those two idiots.

"I know you don't have my daughter around this bitch!" Macy said with fire in her eyes. "She's MY daughter Macy and what the hell do you care, you haven't done a damn thing for Serenity since the day you left! You deadbeat bitch!" Dayton yelled down the aisle. He had finally had enough of Macy and so did I.

"Fuck you Dayton!" Macy yelled back at him. By now someone must have called the police because two officers were walking down the aisle towards us. All of a sudden Macy took off walking quickly down the aisle and away from the police. One of the police officers took off after her and the other officer asked Dayton was everything ok. "That's my soon-to-be ex-wife that took off. I thought she was in jail for nonpayment of child support. She's harassing us while we're trying to shop man." Dayton told the officers.

"I'm going to call a supervisor Dayton, you know it's just procedure." the officer said. The other officer caught up with Macy and walked her back over to where we were. "He pulled his gun out on me!" Macy told the officers. Just completely lying. Of course Dayton was denying it because it wasn't true. We all became engaged in a huge disagreement which was getting out of hand again. After about five minutes the supervising officer arrived. The original officers took the supervisor to the side and began to talk to her. Then they all called Dayton over and then I was called. They asked each one of us individually what happened. I don't know what Macy said to them, but they asked Dayton if he had his duty gun or any other gun on him. "It's in the car Sgt. Meyers. It's not on my person." He said to his Sergeant. "Sgt. Meyers, she said he pulled it out in the store one of the officers said to Dayton's supervisor. The Sergeant and the officers began speaking to some of the other customers that were witnesses to the incident. They all agreed that Dayton never pulled out a gun. "Now she's trying to get my gun taken from me." Dayton said becoming more furious at this point. Evan stood by looking lost and confused. Macy wouldn't shut up yelling that Dayton did pull out his gun and everyone was lying on her. After all of the commotion was over, the officers ran all of our names to see if we had warrants. I myself and Evan all came back clean, but Macy had a few traffic warrants out of Plainfield, Newark and some other places that were not taken care of while she was on her county vacation. So, off to jail she went again. That's why her ass tried to run when she saw the cops coming. Dayton was relieved that he didn't have his gun on him at that moment. "Thank God I took it off when I was putting Serenity in the car." Dayton said. He looked so tired and frustrated. Instinctively I put my arms around him and gave him a kiss on the cheek. Evan turned and walked away from us. The sergeant and the officers dismissed us all and left to take Macy back to jail. Evan's kids were trying to say goodbye to me but Evan pulled them away. It hurt me for them to have to witness what happened between all of us but it was nothing I could do. I was almost positive that Evan was going to the police station to bail Macy out, but he got in his car and went in the other direction. Dayton and I got the items we needed from Walgreens and headed up to Shoprite to get the stuff I needed to make dinner. Out of the blue Dayton just spoke to me."Saniya he said."

"Yes Dayton." I replied.

"If I ask you a question can you promise me no matter what that you will tell me the truth?"

"Of course I'll tell you the truth Dayton."

"Did you burn down Evan's store?"

The Sum of My Mistakes

Chapter Twenty

Macy

"I'm telling you officers; Dayton Long pulled his gun out on me!" I tried everything I could to make them believe me, but they just wouldn't. So what I was telling a lie, Dayton was a dumbass and he needs to pay for fucking around with Saniya. Now I'm headed back to jail again for no fucking reason. It's cool though, I know Evan will come to the police station and bail me out.

I almost had Evan completely convinced that it was Saniya that burned down his store, until we had to run into her ass at Walgreens. Evan is in love with that stupid bitch and now I have to do whatever I have to kill that love or kill her ass. When I showed up on Evan's door claiming I had nowhere to go, he had to let me in. I just wish his fucking kids didn't have to be around all the time. That shit is annoying. I don't have my own damn child around me why in the fuck would I want anyone else's kids around? I want Evan Roberts to myself but not with all this kid baggage. I can't stand kids. I have to figure out a way to get these fucking kids out of our house. I know it's only been a day but I'm not going anywhere, Evan's ass is never getting rid of me. I didn't push Asia in the way of that train for nothing. Oh yeah, I pushed Asia's car onto those train tracks to make sure she couldn't get in the way of Evan and me. When I arrived at Evan's door, I was coming back from stashing the car I stole to push her car onto the train tracks. I torched that car in Newark and took the train back to Plainfield. Got off at the Netherwood Station and took a cab to Evan's house. He didn't even know I knew where he lived. I knew after the good ass I gave him that he wouldn't turn me away. I caught him just as he was on his way to the hospital to find out what was going on with Asia. I can't believe that bitch didn't die already. Next bitch I'm going to take out is Saniya. I have to figure out a way to do it and make it look like Dayton had something to do with it. Then I can kill 2 birds with one stone. That will get Evan's brain off of her, and Dayton will get what he deserves for making me move out. His mother and father can raise Serenity. They don't have shit to do anyway. God knows I don't want to have anything to do with her.

I can't believe Saniya's ass is fucking around with Dayton. That bitch has no idea, Once mine, always mine! I may not want him, but I damn sure don't want her to have him.

Dayton is so pitiful. Always got some stray hanging around. Always trying to save some damn body. That's why I left his ass. No balls. Let him tell it, he put me out, but truth be told, I left him and Serenity to live my own damn life. They were both smothering me. I knew when she came out looking like him I wouldn't have anything to do with her for long. I don't need anything holding me down especially not a man and a kid.

We just arrived at the police station. "Officers can one of you please ask if someone is here to bail me out yet." "Miss, you can ask all of that once we get you inside." "The officer driving said to me. He was brown skinned, very tall brother. The other shorter police officer got out of the car and opened my door to let me out. "So, you're Dayton's wife huh?" "Something like that." I replied.

They took me through the doors leading to the area I was to be booked in. I just knew Evan was there to get me already, so I asked the officer that was booking me did anyone come in to bail me out. He said no one had called or come in, in reference to me. I went through the booking process and received my bail amount, $500 Failure to appear in S. Plainfield, $250 Speeding ticket in Plainfield, $140 Parking ticket in Newark, $1,000 failure to appear in Westfield and a few more. One of the police officers that were on the other side of the booking area came and put me into a cell. "This is some bullshit!" I said out loud in front of the female officer. She was neither moved nor amused by my comment. I tried calling Evan again for the 5th. time and again I got no answer. I know if I try to call Dayton he'll hang up on me. I had nowhere to go and no one else to call. I was stuck. What in the fuck am I gonna do now?

The Sum of My Mistakes

Chapter Twenty-One

Evan

So I guess that bullshit is official. Dayton and Saniya looked like a couple

today. He was holding her hand and playing her protector. I was shocked

as hell to see them at Walgreens together. My dumb ass had to take that

fucking Macy with me. I know it's not going to help me get Saniya back

hanging around with Macy's ass. I had a feeling when she asked me if she

could go to Walgreens that she was going to be a damn problem. When

she showed up at my door...I know I should have called the police, but I

felt sorry for her stupid ass and she agreed to drop the charges against me.

I asked her why she lied about saying I sexually assaulted her and she said

she was just upset and she knows she was wrong. I can't believe she told

the police that Dayton pulled his gun out on her, knowing it was a

complete lie. I see a lie can fall out of her mouth at any time. I don't need

to have her around my kids if she lies like that. I don't think my kids like her too much anyway. I know they are going through a lot right now with their mother being in such a bad accident and them being thrown into staying with me. I haven't seen them in a few months and I don't know what's going on with them or even how to talk to them. Isis just wants her mom and Little Evan won't even look at me. I have to let Macy stay at my house until she can go to the police department and drop those charges against me. I can't take the risk of her not dropping the charges and I'll end up having to pay out a bunch of money to my lawyers. I just can't do that right now. I have too much going on financially. Then there's him. Through all of this nonsense I haven't even been able to tell Saniya or anyone else about him. My life seems to be going to hell. One stupid thing after another is happening to me. I don't know why but I need to figure this shit out.

Three months ago I got a friend request on Face Book from a one Ethan Roberts. My brother. I didn't even know I had a brother. The only sibling I ever knew I had was my sister Lilly who passed away when I was 13 years old. I was raised as an only child. With a single mother and a father that stopped by to get some ass from my mother when he felt like it but somehow seemed to forget that I even existed. I never got so much as a "hi" from him when I did see him. Usually the only way I even knew he was there was when I heard mama's headboard banging against the wall on the other side of my wall. That's when I realized he was in the house. I longed for that man my entire life and was no damn where to be found. Now all of a sudden he shows up asking me for a kidney for my brother. This brother I never even knew I had. That's straight up bull. This man never showed me any type of love. This man treated me and my mother like shit. Now he has the nerve to want to get in touch with me because my brother will die if he doesn't get a kidney from me. What makes them think I'm a match for Ethan anyway? I've had this shit on my mind for 3 months now. The old bastard never even asked me how I was, just straight in with the questions about my kidney. I wanted to speak to him like he was a piece of crud under my shoe, but my mother always made me show this deadbeat the utmost respect. So I politely told him to please not ever call me again. He hung up on me. About ten minutes later Ethan, my brother literally from another mother called me sounding desperate.

Ring….Ring…Ring… "Hello." I hesitated answering the phone.

"Hello, may I speak to Evan Roberts please." The voice on the other end of the phone sounded like my voice.

"This is Evan Roberts speaking. Who is this?"

"Evan, this is your brother, Ethan."

"Hello Ethan." I said politely.

"Evan, I don't know what went on with you and dad, but man I'm just asking for a chance to live." Ethan begged.

"That's your father, not mine." I replied.

"I feel what you're saying Evan, but please can you just listen to dad this once." Ethan begged again. I made up a quick excuse to hang up with Ethan and dismissed both phone calls. The anger I felt for my father wouldn't allow me to even hear what this stranger, my brother, was saying. All I could hear was my father's voice telling me to give this gift to this man who shares half of my DNA and my last name. I refused to even listen to them plead their case. Once I knew my father was involved, that was it for me. The answer was no. absolutely NO! I've been living with that decision ever since. Guilt has eaten me alive. I'm too afraid to call that sperm donor of mine back, just in case the stranger with my last name, Ethan Roberts didn't make it.

My phone began to ring and it jolted me back to the present. Ring...Ring...Ring...."Same number, not answering it, I know its Macy again. This girl just can't get the hint. "I'M NOT COMING TO GET YOU!!" I said out loud. "Daddy who are you talking to?" Little Evan

158

asked me. His voice snapped me out of the trance I was in. "Nobody son." I lied.

Ring...Ring....Ring...My phone rang again. I'm not answering this shit. Again... more than likely it's Macy's ass and I'm not going to bail her out. I'll just have to fight her charges against me in court. Too much on my mind and I'm not taking my kids to no jail to bail her out. I'm not exposing them to that. "Daddy, why does your phone keep ringing?" Evan asked me. "I think they have the wrong number." I lied to him.

Ring...Ring...Ring...my phone rang yet again. This time it was area code 252 that flashed across my screen. That's Ethan's area code, but not his number. Damn it, should I answer? I thought to myself. I was scared to death to answer. Maybe it was someone calling to tell me that Ethan had passed away. On the other hand I was so sick of hearing my phone ring, I just hit the answer button and said Hello. "Hello?" I said very quietly and with caution. "Hello may I speak to Evan Roberts please." The female voice on the other end of the phone was soft and weak. I was thrown off by it being a female on the phone. I was expecting Ethan or my sperm donor to be on the other end. "This is Evan Roberts speaking; who may I ask is calling?" I said trying to put some authority in my voice. "My name is Heaven Roberts, my father is Ethan Roberts." "Hello Heaven, what can

I do for you?" I said my voice softening. "I'm calling you because my dad has taken a turn for the worse and I was wondering if there was any way that you could find it in your heart to come visit him, he would really like to meet you before he passes." Damn! He really is that sick. I thought to myself.

"I don't know if that's possible Heaven."

"Uncle Evan please, it's not daddy's fault that he never contacted you before. He just found out about you three months ago when my grandpa finally told him about you." Well that answered one of my questions, If Ethan knew about me all of these years. He didn't. Well I guess my sperm donor kept me a secret from Ethan like he kept Ethan a secret from me. No shocker, hell my father kept his entire life a secret from me. That bastard. Anyway, I thought about it for a brief second and then answered Heaven's question. "Heaven let me see if I can find a sitter for my kids and check on a few things. Then I'll call you back and let you know if I can come. I'm not saying no, I'm just saying give me a few days and I'll get back to you." I figured Heaven would say ok and we would end our call, but that wasn't the case. "Uncle Evan, my dad may not have a few days." Heaven snapped. At that moment I think it finally hit me how serious this was. I fucked up. I could have possibly saved this man's life but because of the hate I have for my father, Ethan is going to lose his life. I quickly re-evaluated what I'd done. I decided I had to go. "Ok Heaven, text me the address and I'll make arrangements to be there. Heaven is this your cell number?" "Yes it is"... Heaven said with more enthusiasm in her voice than when she first called. "Ok Heaven, I'll call you back in a few hours. I may have to bring my kids, is that ok?"

"Yes of course Uncle Evan." Heaven's enthusiasm was fueling my determination to meet my brother before he passed away. "Good bye and thank you Uncle Evan."

"Good bye Heaven, hopefully I'll get to meet you very soon."

"Looking forward to it." and with that Heaven hung up. I clicked 'end call' on my phone and immediately began to think what I could do with the kids. I honestly didn't want to leave them, but I didn't want them to experience watching two people possibly pass away.

I pulled into the driveway of my house and looked around cautiously to see if Macy might have gotten out and was lurking in the bushes. I didn't see anyone, so the kids and I got out of the car and went into the house. I checked to see if I had any messages on the house phone and there were no messages and no new numbers on the caller id. I put down my purchases from Walgreens and asked the kids if they were hungry. Of course they said yes. Thank God Saniya always kept the house stocked with food. I pulled a few frozen dinners out and read the directions on how long they needed to be in the microwave. I made the dinners and fed the kids. I had promised them I would take them to see their mom today so I told them to get ready to go to the hospital. They told me they were tired and they wanted to take a nap first so they went upstairs to their bedrooms to take a little nap. That gave me a few minutes to figure out what I could do about this trip to North Carolina. I called Asia's sister to see if the kids could stay with her for a few days and although she gave me attitude on the phone she agreed to let the kids stay. I got online, booked a flight for myself for tomorrow afternoon and started packing up some stuff for the trip. I booked a rental car and a hotel for as close as I could to the address Heaven had given me. Because of all the madness that had been going on the past few days, I really did need to get away. This would give me some time to do some thinking. My phone began to ring again.... this time it was that same number that was calling me ever since Macy got arrested. I hit the ignore button and went back to packing. I thought of Saniya the entire time I was packing. I wish she could go on this trip with me. I could really use her positive spirit and her strength. Damn... I can't believe I fucked our relationship up so badly. Not going to dwell on that right now. She

162

obviously bounces back really quickly. Anyway, The insurance company was coming the next morning to inspect the Plainfield building and then I could leave for two or three days but not much longer.

After I was mostly packed, I sat down for a minute to catch a breather. I guess I must have drifted off to sleep because the next thing I knew someone was ringing my doorbell and knocking on my door. I just knew Macy's ass got out and was at my door once again. I didn't want to answer the door but my car was in the driveway so it was obvious I was home. Annoyed, I walked down the steps and up to the door and yelled "Who is it?" I got no response at first from the other side of the door. I snatched open the door and almost had a heart attack. "It's me Evan, your father!"

The Sum of My Mistakes

Chapter Twenty-Two

Dayton

Damn running into Evan didn't go over well at all. The sight of Macy makes me sick. I can't believe I ever married that girl. Everybody tried to tell me not to but I wouldn't listen. Now I have this beautiful woman Saniya in my presence and it's been constant drama. Saniya told me to keep on driving when we got to Walgreens but I wasn't hearing that. Evan Roberts is not going to move any mountains in my life. I must admit, he looked really hurt when he saw me with Saniya. I'm not trying to hurt a brother but there's just something about Saniya that I can't let go of. Ever since the day I met her I'm really feeling her. I know she's going through some things but I know if I just stay here by her side things will be ok eventually. She bonded so well with Serenity and she cooks her ass off. What more could I ask for?

I know the guys at work are going to have a field day when I go back tomorrow. I can't believe Macy tried to say that I pulled my gun out on her in a store full of people. She's completely out of her mind. If I was going to pull my gun out on her ass I would have done it a long time ago. She didn't even ask about Serenity. That's sad as hell. How could I have chosen such a horrible person to be my child's mother? How could I have married such a poor excuse for a woman? I could ask myself those questions all damn day and night, but the bottom line was I had a daughter I had to take care of. No matter what I was a single father.

Saniya didn't talk to me the entire ride to Shoprite and back to her and Jae'mi's house. She barely spoke to me during the fantastic dinner she cooked. But she took care of Serenity like she was hers and I was extremely impressed. I tried joking with her and teasing her but nothing worked. Jae'mi must have felt the tension because soon after dinner she took Azera and Serenity upstairs so Saniya and I could be alone. "Saniya what's wrong?" I asked almost positive I already knew the answer to my question. "Nothing Dayton." Saniya responded without even looking at me. She had completely shut down and I knew there was nothing I could do. I didn't know if it was the altercation that occurred between us, Evan and Macy, the fact that she saw Evan's kids and it got to her or my question of whether or not she burned down Evan's store. Deep down I knew it was the latter of the three situations. I tried to apologize but she wasn't hearing it. "Saniya if you're mad at me for asking you if you burned down the store, I'm sorry, I just needed to hear you say no."

"Why Dayton?" she snapped. "Why would you ask me something like that? What type of person do you think I am?" She said with anger in her voice. I felt so stupid that I had ever asked her that question. There was no way Saniya set fire to anything and I should have figured that out before I opened my mouth.

"Saniya, I'm so sorry... I said as I walked up to her to hug her, but she turned her back to me. I wrapped my arms around her and held her anyway. She tensed up at first but then she began to relax. I turned her around to face me and looked into her eyes. "Damn you're beautiful." I whispered to her.

"Thank you." she said dryly.

"Saniya I'm trying to apologize to you, I'm sorry for even asking you if you burned down that store. I know you would never do a thing like that. Saniya can you forgive me?" I put on the sad face as I asked for her

166

forgiveness. She didn't want to say she forgave me at first, but I think I got her with the sad face.

"Yeah I forgive you silly!" Saniya broke out a smile and laughed at my pitiful sad face act. "Don't ever make that face again!" she said as she playfully tapped me on my chest.

"I know you just hit me to catch a quick feel." I said laughing. This made Saniya crack up. I just stared into her eyes and watched her laugh. I was in awe of this woman I hardly knew. Saniya stopped laughing and stared right back at me. I bent over a little and gave her a peck on the lips. I just wanted to make sure she was ready for me to kiss her. She smiled nervously at me but she didn't push me away. I gently pulled her close to me and then I kissed her passionately. Saniya hesitated at first but finally kissed me back. I couldn't believe she actually kissed me back. I stood there holding her for a few minutes. I rested my head on hers and just stood there and held her and she held me back.

The doorbell rang and Saniya let me go and went to answer the door. I turned around and watched her walk over to the door. She asked "Who is it." And she opened the door and there stood some light skinned brother with hazel eyes. "What in the fuck are you doing here?" Saniya yelled.

"Wait, Saniya, don't close the door!" the guy yelled as Saniya slammed the

167

door and ran to me crying. "Saniya who in the hell was that?" I said

realizing I didn't have my gun on me.

"That was Sebastian the guy that raped me!"

The Sum of My Mistakes

Chapter Twenty-Three

Saniya

OMG I almost passed out when I opened the door. How in the hell did Sebastian know where I was? Was he watching me? I'm so glad Dayton was here. Jae'mi might have shot Sebastian if she had answered the door and saw who it was. I slammed the door and ran to Dayton when I saw Sebastian. I didn't know what to do. Dayton called the police for me and took off running outside to find Sebastian. Jae'mi came running down the stairs. "Saniya, what the hell happened who was at the door?"

"That was Sebastian at the door."

"What!?" Jae'mi said reaching for her gun on her hip and the door at the same time. Dayton came back in the house as Jae'mi reached for the door handle. "I didn't see him, Saniya; did you see which way he went?"

"No, Dayton I didn't. I was scared out of my mind." I said trembling all over.

"Calm down Saniya, everything's going to be ok." Dayton said trying to calm me down. As Dayton turned to close the door two squad cars pulled up and three officers got out. "Where'd he go Dayton?" One of the officers yelled from the street.

"Man I don't know. It's like he just disappeared." Dayton responded.

"Well Dayton, tell me what happened man" The officer said

"My lady friend was attacked the other night and her attacker just showed up here."

"Is there a restraining order on him?"

"Yes there is, and he's been served."

"What does he look like Dayton? What is he wearing? And what's his name?" The officer with the stripes on his arm asked.

"His name is Sebastian Young, he's about 6' 2", about 200 pounds, light skinned black male with hazel eyes and curly hair." Wow Dayton was good. How did he see all of that in those few seconds?

"He had on a black tee shirt and jeans with tan work boots." I interjected, finally finding some strength to speak. Two of the officers got back into their patrol car and drove off with the lights off. The officer with the stripes, and Dayton ran to the back of the house. "Saniya, I'll be right back I have to check on Azera and the baby." Jae'mi said and headed up the steps. I closed the door and sat down on the couch. I was scared to death. What in the hell did Sebastian come over here for? I wondered to myself. He knows he has a restraining order, what the hell is wrong with him? I decided right then it may not be such a good idea for me to stay here if he knows where I am. What if he comes back and Dayton and or Jae'mi aren't here. What will I do then? What the hell is going on right now!? What in the hell did I do to deserve all of this?

Dayton and the officers came into the house. After a short discussion about what happened and me showing them my part of the restraining order, all of the officers went out to their cars but only the officer with the stripes got in his car and left. The other car stayed in front of the house. Dayton said they were going to do some extra patrol in our area tonight just in case Sebastian came back. "Saniya, I have to take my little angel home and get her ready for bed, are you going to be ok?" Dayton said to me as he began to gather Serenity's things.

"Yeah I guess." I said in a weak tone.

"Saniya I have to be back at work tomorrow morning. I promise you as soon as I get off I'll be right here." Dayton tried to reassure me.

"Dayton, I think I'm going to go stay in a hotel tonight." I said not knowing what else to do.

"You don't need to be alone Saniya, the officers will be here most of the night until they get a call, your sister is here, and Azera doesn't need to be in a hotel." He reasoned.

"I guess you're right." I said not really agreeing with Dayton. Dayton headed up the steps to say goodbye to Sy and Jae'mi and to get Serenity. I went into the kitchen to start loading up the dishwasher and clean up the kitchen. For the life of me, I kept feeling like I was being watched. I locked the back door and closed all of the windows downstairs. Dayton and Jae'mi came down the stairs with Serenity. I helped Dayton finish wrapping her up and kissed her goodbye. Dayton picked up her bag as I strapped her into her car seat. Dayton hugged Jae'mi goodbye and I decided to walk with him out to the car. Dayton put Serenity on the car seat base and put the diaper bag in the car. I noticed that the police car was gone and again I got this crazy feeling that someone was watching me. "Dayton, I feel like someone is watching me." saying what I was thinking out loud.

"Saniya, I promise you, as soon as I get home and get Serenity settled, I'll call you. Your sister is here and she won't leave you alone."

"Ok", I said trying to sound a little stronger. Dayton kissed me on the lips and walked around to the driver's side of the car. "I'll call you in a few

Saniya."

"Ok." I said and I headed back into the house.

I got Azera ready for bed and got my own self in the shower and ready for

bed. I went in Jae'mi's room and climbed onto the foot of her bed. "Jae'mi,

I'm so scared." I said to my sister.

"I know Saniya, but you don't need to be, Dayton and I have your back."

"What about when you're not here?"

"I have something that may help you." Jae'mi said as she got off of her

bed and headed to her closet. Jae'mi pulled out a metal box from the very

back of her closet. She took a small key from her key ring and unlocked

and opened the box. She turned the box around so I could see what was

inside. "Oh Jae'mi, a gun?" I said shocked. "Damn Jae'mi, it's been a long

time since I held a gun." I said as I reached into the box and retrieved the

piece of steel. "This is nice." I said as I examined the 9MM weapon. It's

registered to me it's my off duty weapon. If Sebastian brings his ass back

to this house, you blow his ass away." She said in her stern voice.

"I sure will." I said to Jae'mi.

"I'm going to put it back into this box and give you the other key."

"Sounds like a plan to me girl!" I said. Now I was feeling a little more secure.

I heard my phone ringing in the other room. I just knew it was Dayton, so I ran into the room and got my phone and answered it without even looking at the name on the screen. "Hello." I said with some cheer in my voice.

"Hello Saniya." It wasn't Dayton. It was Sebastian.

"Stop fucking calling me Sebastian." I said, not feeling as scared as I did earlier.

"Why did you press charges on me Saniya?"

"Sebastian, you're a sick bastard, don't ever call my phone again, and if you show up at my door again, I'll fucking kill you! After what you did to me, how fucking dare you try to contact me!"

"I didn't do anything wrong to you Saniya."

"Are you fucking retarded? You drugged me and had sex with me you fucking rapist!" I yelled into the phone.

"You're used to dick Saniya, you were a porn star and a stripper, are you serious, now you have morals?" How dare he bring up my past and use it to justify what he did to me. What a fucking asshole!

"My past is none of your business Sebastian."

"Saniya everything about you is my business, I made you my business." Sebastian said, sounding like a crazy man. Now this damn fool really had himself convinced that what he did to me was ok. How crazy. "Sebastian, I don't care what you're crazy mind thinks. I don't want you, leave me the fuck alone!" I continued to yell into the phone. "Saniya, I'll never leave you alone, you're mine and tell your new boyfriend to watch his back, cause cop or no cop, I will get rid of his ass one way or another." Did he just threaten Dayton?

"Sebastian, leave him out of it."

"Whatever Saniya, does your little boyfriend know about your past?"

"That's none of your business Sebastian!" I was really getting pissed with the comments he was making. "Like I said Saniya, you are my business, and if you don't drop the charges against me, I'm going to tell your little boyfriend ALL of your business." "Fuck you!" I said and then I hung up on Sebastian.

My phone immediately rang again. This time it was Dayton. "Hey Dayton." I said trying not to cry.

"Saniya what's wrong?"

"Sebastian just called me." I confessed.

"What did he say?" Dayton's whole attitude changed when he asked me that. I think he was getting tired of my drama.

"He said a bunch of bullshit. Tomorrow I'm changing my number."

"Good idea Saniya. By the way, I called headquarters to find out if they issued a warrant for Sebastian's re-arrest."

"Thanks Dayton, please tell me they did."

"Yes they did, so next time he contacts you in anyway, call the cops."

"Ok Dayton." I opened the night table drawer and got out the sleeping pills I got from the hospital. I opened the bottle and took out one of the pills.

"So Saniya, what are you getting ready to do now?"

"I'm getting ready to take it down." I said in my getting sleepy voice. "What time do you have to be at work in the morning Dayton?"

"Five o'clock."

"Damn, you need to go to bed it's one in the morning."

"I know, but I had to make sure you were ok." "Aww...thank you Dayton, but you can go to bed, I'm ok." I really wasn't, but I had to keep my head so I can figure out what to do about Sebastian.

I didn't have anything to drink to take my sleeping pill so I walked down stairs, went in the kitchen and I got myself some juice. I popped one of my pills in my mouth and took a swallow of juice. I was still on the phone with Dayton and I got that feeling again. "Dayton I still have the feeling that someone is watching me."

"Where are you Saniya?"

"I'm in the kitchen."

"Check all of the windows and doors and go upstairs and get in the bed. Don't sleep in the living room tonight."

"Ok." I said agreeing with him. "Dayton, go ahead and go to bed, I'll talk to you in the morning."

"Good night Saniya."

"Good night Dayton." Click. I hung up the phone. I was getting ready to walk up the steps and back into the room and go to bed, but there was a tap at the front door. "Who the hell is it?" I yelled at the door nervous as hell. I just knew it was Sebastian's ass again. Then I heard his voice."It's me Evan. Saniya, please open the door."

The Sum of My Mistakes

Chapter Twenty-Four

Sebastian

Saniya has been quite busy today. Running around all day with that damn cop and now she's in the house talking to Evan. This would be the perfect opportunity to kill Evan's ass but I'm going to wait. Since I got out, I've been trying to talk to Saniya, but all she does is hang up on me. I got her ass to listen tonight though. She's spending all day and night with that cop when she should be spending it with me. I finally got her away from Evan and the way I put this dick on her. She should definitely want to be with me now. I don't understand what the hell her problem is. So what I put a little GHB in her drink, I didn't kill her. Shit always has to be so damn trivial. Now here I am facing these rape charges. Luckily my cousin bailed me out of jail. $2500. Ten percent on $25,000 I'm not going through any trial. Saniya has to drop those charges. I've already done 3 years for possession with intent; I'm not doing 5-10 over no pussy. I had a funny feeling Saniya hadn't told her little boyfriend about her past. Now I can use that bit of information to get me off. Maybe if I play my cards right, I can get some more of that good pussy by using all of the information I have on her. Yeah, let me go home and get a little rest so I can get up nice and early and call me new lady to be Ms. Saniya Wheeler.

The Sum of My Mistakes

Chapter Twenty-Five

Evan

"What in the fuck is he doing here?" I mumbled to myself. I was in disbelief. I opened the door and couldn't believe my eyes. My sperm donor was standing on my front steps. How in the hell did this asshole find me? I thought to myself. I was completely speechless. My heart felt like a ton of bricks and was pounding. I was hoping my eyes were deceiving me. Here I was, face to face with my number one enemy, my father. Evan Emerson Roberts Sr. Yes, I'm a Jr. believe it or not. I never put the Jr. in my name because there was never a Sr. in my life, to be the Jr. of. "What in the hell are you doing here?" I said with fire in my eyes and in my voice. I spoke to him like I was speaking to scum. Like he was the last person I wanted to talk to. Because he was. This was how much respect I had for this so-called man. One thing that was really pissing me off was the fact that he was standing here looking like what I presume I will look like in 20 years. My body, aged 20 years. My eyes and those thin lines I've been seeing when I look in the mirror. My nose, just a bit smaller and more defined. Even my full round lips. I am the spitting image of this so-called father of mine. "That's the way you greet your father Evan Jr?"

Was he fucking serious? I haven't seen this asshole in over forty years, and he was still as cocky as the last day I remember seeing him. I was eight and my mother had just discovered my dad's latest lover was the one who slashed the tires on her car. She had finally had enough of trying to love my father and not getting any love back, so she decided to leave him. My mom packed her bags and gave me a small suitcase to pack my things in also. I put as much as I could in that little suitcase and threw some of my toys into a plastic bag. My mom kept telling me to hurry up so we could leave before my dad got home from work, but I was so nervous packing my things I ended up getting us caught. My father was not happy that my mother was leaving him. That meant he didn't have the opportunity to kick us out. He cursed my mother every way he could. Calling her all types of whores, and sluts. He told her to get her and her bastard child (meaning me) out of his house. He dumped all of my belongings out of the suitcase because the suitcase belonged to him and then he pushed us my mom's and my sister's things out of the front door. That was the last time I ever saw or heard from him.

"Man look, I'm not in the mood for whatever your reason is for being here on my doorstep. You're not welcome here." I told my father. He pushed right past me and into my living room he went, he stood in the middle of the floor demanding I come in and sit down and hear him out.

"Come in Jr and have a seat, I really need for us to talk." I didn't know what to call him; I hated calling him dad because as far as I was concerned, he was no type of father.

"Look man, I'm not interested in whatever it is you have to say, I just want you out of my house!" I raised my voice a little more to get my point across.

"I'm not going anywhere, so call the police, physically put me out, do whatever you feel you have to do, but I'm not leaving until you hear me out Evan Jr.!" My father yelled.

I hated that word, Jr. That just connected me to a man who I damn sure didn't want to be connected to at all, but I decided I didn't need any more cops involved in my life at all, so I closed my front door and walked over to my sofa and took a seat.

"You have 5 minutes." I warned my father. "So start talking now." I said, finally calming down.

"Jr...

---"Please don't call me that." I interrupted whatever it was he was about to say. "Just call me Evan please." I said hoping this was going to be quick and painless.

"Ok, Evan" My father said seeming as frustrated with me as I was with him. "Evan, I'm asking, no I'm begging you to please help your brother Ethan out. He's very sick Evan, and he's seriously going to die soon if somebody doesn't donate their Kidney to him. No matter what's going on with you and me, I really need you to help your brother out Evan." I knew he was right, but my stubbornness wouldn't let me tell him that.

"Look, I hear what you're saying, but I am going through some things right now, and I really can't get away." I told my father, hoping this would be the end of this conversation.

"Damn, I can't believe you're such a selfish man Evan!" My father yelled. I couldn't believe this man said something like that to me!

"Selfish, are you fucking kidding me? Me selfish? How dare you call me selfish after the way you treated me all of these years. It's because of YOU that I didn't even know I had a brother!" I spat at my father.

"No Evan, it's not because of me, it's because of your mother!" He spat back at me.

"Don't you dare put my mother into this!" I spat back.

"Evan, you think your mother is so sweet and innocent, and she's not!" My father yelled.

"I'm telling you right now, leave my mother out of this, don't talk about my mother!" I warned him.

"Evan, your mother told me you were not my son!" He said, then his eyes got big and he looked like he was shocked that he said it to me.

"Stop fucking lying!" I yelled, completely furious and in disbelief. My father had turned his back to me for a brief second and when he turned around, there were tears in his eyes.

"Evan, I'm not lying to you, your mother had an affair." He said with his head hung low.

"What?" I said not wanting to believe him. He repeated it...this time a little more calm he said the words again.

"Evan, your mother had an affair... with my brother, your Uncle Eddie. I sank down into the couch. My mind was racing. I was in utter disbelief.

"Mom and Uncle Eddie?" I said under my breath. God please let this man be lying.

The Sum of My Mistakes

Chapter Twenty-Six

Macy

It's been 3 days and I'm still locked up. I went to see the judge and they're not reducing my bail amount because I was just in court the other day for child support and they already gave me another chance. Either I pay all of the money I owe or I do 30 days, and I'm not doing 30 days! The traffic warrants I had didn't come up when I got arrested for child support, but they came up when they checked me the other day at Walgreens. I thought Evan would have been here to bail me out but he hasn't called, or come in at all. That shit really pisses me off. When I get done with his ass he's going to be in jail for the rest of his fucking life! I have called him at least 50 times and he didn't answer one of my calls. I saw Dayton the other day before they brought me to the county jail and he just smirked when he saw me. He may be laughing now but I'll laugh last I guarantee that.

This cellmate of mine Renee is weird as hell, but she's all I have to talk to right now. I'm not sure what she's in here for. She won't say, but rumor has it she assaulted her boyfriend's mother. I'm not sure if she won the fight or not, but she has a nice big black eye, and she is limping from something.

"Good morning Macy." Renee said to me with a big smile on her face.

"Whatever." I replied back to her. I wasn't in the mood to speak and I wasn't in the mood for the stupid smile Renee had on her face.

"Time to eat." She smirked and headed towards the food line.

"What the fuck is so funny?" I said to Renee.

"It's my last day here, I get out tomorrow." She responded almost giggling.

"Whip de doo." I said with obvious sarcasm in my voice. Suddenly my mind started racing. "Renee where do you live?"

"South Plainfield, why Macy?"

"I may need you to do me a little favor when you get out."

"A favor?"

"Yes a favor, I need you to deliver a letter for me in Plainfield, is that ok with you?"

"Macy, why can't you just mail the letter, wouldn't that be easier?" Renee

186

asked. I sure was not in the mood for her reasoning."

"Look Renee, can you deliver this letter for me or not?" I snapped.

"Ok yes Macy, I'll deliver the letter for you."

"Thanks, I appreciate it." I lied. She better had agreed to do it for me, or I would have sent her ass home bruised the hell up. I was going to get out of here one way or another, and I didn't need the guards reading what I had to write in this letter.

I scarfed down my food and headed right back to my cell to get the letter together. I had to make it a good one with no trace of it coming back to me. If Renee just dropped it off for me, I may have one more option of getting bailed out. The recipient would be sure to come bail me out as soon as he read it. I thought very carefully as to what I was going to put in the letter.

I finally finished writing the letter and waited for Renee to get back to our cell. "Hi Macy, did you finish the letter you need me to drop off for you?" Renee asked me happy as a pig in slop. I was sick to my stomach watching her be all happy and shit.

"Yeah Renee I finished the letter." I handed the letter to Renee and warned her exactly what would happen if she screwed this up and didn't deliver it to the right person. She joyfully put it in her bible and promised she won't screw up. I would hate to hunt her down and do to her what I did to Asia.

I had forgotten to address the outside of the envelope so I asked Renee if I could see the letter again. She reached in her bible and retrieved the letter. I wrote the name and the address on the envelope.

Sebastian Young

1015 West 6th. St.

Plainfield, NJ 07060

I gave Renee the instructions on how to get to Sebastian's house. She knew exactly where it was. So that meant there were to be no excuses as to why the letter wouldn't get to Sebastian. "Again Renee, if you don't deliver this letter to the right person, and it gets into the wrong hands, your ass is mine I warned. Renee didn't seem to have the common sense to be afraid of me, but she should. Like I said, I'd hate for her to have "an accident". "No Macy, it won't be a problem delivering your letter. I'll make sure I deliver it straight to Sebastian." Renee said smiling. She was one stupid looking chick. I just really hate her smile and the fact that she was getting out tomorrow instead of me. Shit really pissed me off.

I walked to the phones and attempted to call Evan again. Why I have no idea, he won't answer any of my phone calls. It's obvious. He's not going to come and get me. He's just going to keep ignoring my calls. When I do get out, I'm going to make sure I stick to my story about him sexually assaulting me. I would have dropped the charges, but he left me no choice. If Evan thinks he can just sleep with me and walk away, he's absolutely out of his mind. No way in the world I'm going to let go of him. No fucking way!

It was time for us to go to our cells and go to bed. I was so over excited about the letter I'd written and the possibility of me getting out soon I couldn't sleep. Renee was knocked out and snoring rather loudly. I sat up in my bunk and thought about what I was going to do when Sebastian came to get me. How I was going to juggle him and Evan until the baby got here. My little plan to carry Sebastian's child and tell Evan it was his, was slowly falling apart. The only time Evan and I ever had sex, we used a few condoms. There's no way in the world he was going to think the baby I was carrying was his. I needed a slip up. Just one time for Evan and I to sleep together without protection. I'm already 4 weeks pregnant so this has to happen ASAP. I still don't want any kids, but I'll use this baby to get and keep Evan. Sebastian is just the sperm donor. I'll get rid of his ass quick, fast and in a hurry. Yes he will definitely have a little "accident" that he won't survive. I have a lot of thinking and planning to do, so I need to get some rest. I have to wake up bright and early in the morning to see Renee off, and to make sure she delivers my letter. Freedom here I come!!!

The Sum of My Mistakes

Chapter Twenty-Seven

Saniya

I really didn't think it was him at first. I had to ask again "Who is it?"

"Saniya, it's me Evan, please open the door." I hesitated but then decided

to open the door.

"What is it Evan?" I stood in the doorway not sure if I was going to let

him in. That's until I saw the tears in his eyes. "Evan, what happened?

What's wrong?" I asked. I was very concerned. In all the time I knew

Evan, I had never seen him cry. I knew it had to be very serious not only

because of the tears, but because he had taken the risk of coming over to

Jae'mi's house at this time of night.

"Saniya, can I please come in?"

"Yes, of course I said to Evan as I stepped aside to let him in. Evan

stepped into the house and tears were streaming down his face. I gave him a minute to get himself together, then I invited him to sit down on the couch and I sat in the chair across from him and handed him some tissue that were on the side table. Evan cleaned his face and blew his nose. He took a deep breath and began to speak. "Saniya, my father is at my house."

"What? Your father? What is he doing at your house Evan? I thought you didn't get along with your father.

I didn't even think you knew where your father was."

"I didn't. I haven't heard from him in over 30 years." He said beginning to tear up again.

"Well what's going on Evan? What does your father want and why are you so upset?"

"Saniya he told me he may not be my father. He said my mother had an affair with his brother and I may be his nephew and not his son."

"What!?" I said. I was stunned. I couldn't believe what I was hearing. I sat there waiting for Evan to continue his story. He just sat there, looking dazed and confused. "Evan, your father came to NJ just to tell you that you were not his son?"

"No, he came here to convince me to give my brother Ethan one of my kidneys."

"Brother?" again I was stunned. "You have a brother?"

"Yes, apparently my father got re-married and had another son, well had a son I mean."

"Wow!" Was all I could say.

"Then Evan continued. "If I don't give Ethan my kidney, he will die. I'm his last and final hope"

"Really? There's nobody else that can help him?" I asked Evan.

"No apparently he has this very rare blood type that nobody seems to be able to match.

"Evan I'm so sorry to hear all of this." I said. I was genuinely concerned for Evan; he didn't look like he was taking any of this news very well.

"Saniya, bad thing is, it may already be too late for me to save him.

"Oh God that's so sad. Suddenly I realized the kids weren't with him.

"Evan, where are the kids?" I asked.

"They're with Asia's sister, I just dropped them off." He replied. "I'm going to NC in the afternoon, to meet my, umm brother, well Ethan."

"That's a good idea Evan. What are you going to do about your father?"

"I don't know Saniya. On one hand he's telling me I need to give my brother my kidney and on the other hand he's saying he may not be my father. I don't know what to believe or what to do at this point."

"I can understand that." I assured Evan.

193

"I'm going to go to NC and get tested to find out if I'm a match for my brother Ethan, and then I guess my so-called father and I need to take a DNA paternity test."

"Yes, that's a good idea Evan."

"Saniya he told me stuff about my mother that I just can't believe. He shattered every good feeling I had for my mother. I don't know what to think about her now."

"Evan, have you spoken to your mother since he told you what he told you?"

"No, I don't know what to say to her."

"Well, you can't judge her from what your father says you have to remember the woman she showed you she is."

"You're right Saniya; I'm going to go visit her when I get through handling my business in NC."

"That's a great idea, and when you go to talk to her remember to listen to her also."

"I will." he replied.

The pill I took was starting to really kick in. I suddenly got so sleepy

I could see that Evan was feeling much better.

"Thank you Saniya."

"You're welcome Evan."

"Wow, you look mighty sleepy Saniya. I guess I'll go now." He said as he stood up to leave.

"Yes, you have a lot to do and a lot to think about." I said. "Yes, I do."

All of a sudden there was a knock at my door. "Who is it?" I asked, scared it would be Sebastian again. No one responded. Knock...Knock... "I said who is it?" I said a little louder than the first time. Again, no answer. Evan snatched the door open and to my surprise there stood Dayton in the doorway. Oh shit.

The Sum of My Mistakes

Chapter Twenty-Eight

Dayton

When I parked across the street from Jae'mi's house I couldn't believe it. Evan's car was parked in front of the house. I had been calling Saniya for the past hour and got no answer. I didn't know what to think so I ran over here worried something had happened to her, Azera or even Jae'mi. I woke up my mom so she could watch Serenity for me, and I headed over to make sure the ladies were all ok. I get to the house and Evan's ass is there. At first I started to just go back home and act like I never saw him there, but my heart propelled me to get out of my car and knock on the door. Evan snatched the door open and Saniya stood behind him looking like she had seen a ghost. "Saniya, are you ok?" I pushed past Evan and walked straight up to her.

Saniya tried to explain herself to me, but I wasn't trying to hear it. She didn't owe me an explanation, we are not a couple. I didn't want Evan to think he had me worried about him, so after she said she was ok I just left and went home. I needed to get some sleep for work at 5:00 am.

I tried to sleep for a few hours until I had to work, but I just kept thinking about Saniya and Evan at the front door together. She tried calling me but I didn't answer the phone. I honestly didn't feel like talking. I have serious trust issues with women after the bullshit Macy did to me.

It started very early in our marriage. Macy started messing around with our neighbor upstairs. A much older man named Marcus. She started saying she was going upstairs to help him because he was a sick man who was on his own and he needed help cooking and cleaning his house. She claimed he offered her some money to help him out so of course I agreed. Macy was always a bit selfish so I thought it was a good thing that she wanted to help someone else out for a change. I even ran upstairs sometimes and helped him out myself. That would all come back to bite me on the ass.

I already knew Macy was pregnant when we got married. That's half the reason why I married her. One day I got home a little early from work. I expected Macy to be lying on the bed being lazy as usual but when I came through the door she wasn't there. I tried calling her cell phone, but it was on the kitchen counter when I called it. I figured she couldn't be too far away from home so I decided to check Marcus' house. I went up the stairs and approached Marcus' door and I heard him moaning loudly through the door. I felt a little awkward standing outside the door listening, so I decided to knock. I went to knock and the door came open enough for me to see inside. There was Macy on her knees giving Marcus a blowjob. I stood there stunned for a minute and watched Macy's head in Marcus' hands as he pumped her head up and down on his manhood. Another guy walked into the room stark naked and started to position himself behind Macy's naked body until he saw me standing in the doorway. Macy looked up at me with Marcus' dick in her mouth and yelled to me "Dayton, it's not what you think!" I backed up out of the doorway and ran back downstairs to my apartment. I ran straight into the bathroom and threw up in the toilet. Macy came racing into the house putting her clothes on and screaming my name. "Dayton, it's not what it looks like!" she tried to reason with me. I was so disgusted by what I saw I just demanded immediately that she get the fuck out! She was carrying my child and was having sex with two men at the same time. I found out later that Marcus was paying Macy to have sex with him and his friend on the regular. I wanted to kill his old ass, but I knew it would ruin my career and I would ultimately lose my daughter in the process. I just couldn't let Macy raise my daughter by herself. After a few months of her living from place to place it was almost time for her to give birth. She was completely homeless because everyone managed to throw her out of their homes because of her horrible behavior. I agreed to let her come back home and try to make this so-called marriage work. She went into labor about a week after I let her back in. She tried to act like she had some sense for a while, but I didn't like the way she was treating Serenity. She didn't want to bathe her, she was half ass feeding her and she wasn't interested in bonding with her at all. One day I was at work and I got a call from my mom. She was in the area and stopped by my apartment to see Serenity. She rang the doorbell and Macy came to the door with Serenity on her hip smoking a joint. After I calmed the hell down and got off of work early, I went home and threw Macy out for good. I had her charged with possession and got full custody of my daughter. That was a few months ago. I've been a single father ever since. Best move I could have ever made.

Dam it's time for me to get up for work. I'm tired as hell but I have to do what I have to do. I'm glad Serenity slept with my parents last night. Although I didn't get any sleep, It gave me a chance to think about some things. I'm going to have to seriously talk to Saniya when I get off of work.

The Sum of My Mistakes

Chapter Twenty-Nine

Evan

I left Saniya's house feeling like shit. All of the bullshit I did to her and she still sat there and listened to me. I know she couldn't believe what I was telling her about my mom and Big Evan. Hell, I couldn't believe what Big Evan was telling me about my mother. She actually had an affair with his brother. A full out 3 year affair. He doesn't know if I belong to him or to my uncle Eddie, who I haven't seen in a few years. Uncle Eddie had always kept in touch with me. Until he got sick a few years ago with cancer. He was always trying to be a part of my life. I couldn't understand why my uncle Eddie always made the effort Big Evan never did.

I always saw Uncle Eddie as a pretty good man. Always trying to help me and mama out whenever he could. Always trying to help us make ends meet. Now I know why. He must have felt some type of guilt for the things he had done with my mother.

I had a good meeting with the insurance company. They inspected my burned building and it's looking good that they're going to pay my claim. Still no say in who set the fire. I still don't know what to think. I know that Macy was doing a good job at convincing me that Saniya set that fire. Maybe it's because she was really the person who set the fire. Hopefully one day I'll find out the truth.

I boarded my flight to Rocky Mount. NC. I was both nervous and excited to meet my "brother." My flight landed in NC at 6:48pm. I went to the baggage claim and retrieved my luggage. I headed to the street to see if I could find Heaven who was picking me up. I tried to just get a rental car, but Heaven insisted that she pick me up from the airport. I was standing outside for about 5 minutes when this beautiful young lady with long black hair and my facial features walked straight up to me "Uncle Evan!"

"Heaven?" I asked even though I knew it was her. I couldn't believe she looked so much like me. Wow, if she looks like me I can imagine what Ethan looks like. I thought to myself. "How was your flight Uncle Evan?"

"It was cool." I answered her.

"Would you like to go to the hospital first or would you like to stop by the house and drop off your things?"

"I reserved a hotel room Heaven, I didn't want to impose."

"No Uncle Evan, please don't stay at a hotel, we have plenty of room at the house, and we'd love for you to stay with us." She said. She seemed like such a sweet young lady.

"Ok, I'll stay at your house, but I'd like to go straight to the hospital to meet your dad." I decided to do it and get it over with.

"Okay, we'll be there in a few minutes.

"Thanks Heaven."

"So Uncle Evan, tell me a little about you."

"Well, I'm sort of a single father of two kids a boy and a girl Isis & Evan. Their mother was in an extremely bad car accident a few days ago. She's in intensive care and she's not expected to live.

"Oh my!" Heaven said shocked.

Yeah, sad story. Her car was hit by a train.

"That's crazy Uncle Evan."

"Yes it is Heaven. Anyway, I own my own business. A restaurant distribution company. I'm a chef, have been for twenty years and I just

203

found out that I have a brother and a niece." I said, trying to bring some laughter to the conversation. Heaven let out a little giggle.

"Tell me something about you Heaven."

"Well, I'm 26; I'm working on my master's degree in child psychology. I'm an only child, I'm a daddy's girl and I love to shop." She made me laugh a little. She's got that honest.

I like Heaven, she's very direct and she has a strong personality. "So, tell me about your dad Heaven." Suddenly she started to tear up.

"He's the best father anyone could ever ask for. He doesn't deserve what he's going through right now. He's a provider, a stand up citizen, a great man. He's an excellent and savvy business man. He's made his share of mistakes, but he's overcome all of his downfalls. An unbelievable human being. That's why he deserves his chance to live Uncle Evan. I thought about her description Heaven gave of Ethan and wondered what my kids would say if anyone ever asked them about me. I'm sure I would never get a description quite like that one. As a matter of fact, I would probably get the total opposite description.

Immediately, I started to feel bad. I had waited 3 months to come to NC to meet Ethan Roberts. All because I was being stubborn and pigheaded. I hope it's not too late for me to save his life.

We arrived at Nash Hospital and I became extremely nervous. I didn't know what to say to Heaven after she told me how she felt about her father, so I just sat quietly in the car and didn't say a word.

Heaven parked the car and it was time to get out and go inside the hospital. I hesitated for a second, but then overcame my fears and got out of the car. We walked into the hospital and Heaven waved to the security guard and the people at the information desk. We walked right over to the elevators and went to the Intensive Care Unit, Room 323. We walked into Ethan's room. He was barely awake when we walked in. He was in a lot of pain and they had given him some strong pain medication. "Daddy, Uncle Evan is here." Heaven whispered into Ethan's ear. He opened his eyes and managed to smile a little.

"Ethan, it's so great to meet you." I said as I stared into his eyes. He looked just like a younger me. Everything was the same, his nose, his lips and even the lines around his eyes. He was just smaller in frame and he had fewer gray hairs. "Wow, you look just like me." I said shocked at the resemblance. A tear ran down his cheek and he pulled his hand up to remove the oxygen mask that was on his face.

"Evan, good to finally see you." He managed to say. At that moment Ethan's doctor walked into the room.

"Oh wow, you must be Evan Roberts." He said as he extended his hand to shake mine.

"Yes Doctor?"

"Holmes, Dr. Thomas Holmes" he interjected.

"Good to meet you Dr. Holmes." I said as I shook his hand.

"Good to meet you too Mr. Roberts." Dr. Holmes said to me. "Wow, you two look just alike." Dr. Holmes stared at me in amazement.

"Oh yeah, I know. I agreed. Dr. Holmes turned his attention from me and said hello to Heaven. Then he walked over and spoke to Ethan. "Ethan, how are we feeling today?"

"Not too good doc." Ethan responded.

"Well, I'm going to check you out a little bit Ethan and then tomorrow I want to send you to dialysis. I also want you to have more blood work done.

"Ok doc." Was all that Ethan could manage to say. Doctor Holmes turned to leave and I caught him just as he reached the door.

"Dr. Holmes may I speak to you in the hallway?" I asked not wanting to have this discussion in front of Heaven and Ethan.

"Of course Mr. Roberts." Dr. Homes replied.

Dr. Holmes and I walked out into the hallway and I closed the door behind us. "Dr. Holmes, is there still time to save my brother's life? I asked hoping he would say yes.

"Well, to be honest Mr. Roberts, I'm not sure if there's anything anyone can do for him now. Both of his kidneys have completely shut down and still there's been no one to match his very rare blood type. I felt so bad tears began to form in my eyes. Dr. Holmes must have seen the guilt all over my face. He immediately grabbed my arm and said "Let's see if you're a match first Mr. Roberts"

"Ok cool, but please call me Evan Dr. Holmes."

The Sum of My Mistakes

Chapter Thirty

Saniya

"Yes Dayton, I'm fine." I said trying to see if he was at all upset about Evan being here. If he was upset, he never said a word.

"Thanks for listening Saniya, Evan said as he made his way out of the door. Dayton just watched Evan as he walked out of the house and to his car, neither man acknowledged the other. Evan got into his car and sped off. Dayton turned himself around to leave and I stopped him. "Dayton, it's not what you think." I pleaded

"Saniya, it's none of my business." With that statement, he got into his truck and left. I closed the door after Dayton left and walked over to the couch and sat down. Suddenly I heard "I think you fucked up Saniya.

I looked up and saw Jae'mi standing on the stairs.

"I think I did too." I agreed with her.

I lay down in the bed and tried to go to sleep, but I couldn't. All I could think about was Dayton and the look on his face when he left. He looked hurt and betrayed. I know we're not in any type of relationship, but I know Dayton has feelings for me. Maybe I shouldn't have let Evan in tonight. But I didn't do anything wrong, I just listened to what Evan had to say. Dayton is sure to understand that.

I picked up my cell phone and dialed Dayton's number. It rang three times and then went to voicemail. I left a message "Hey Dayton, it's Saniya, I just wanted to say hi and make sure you and I are ok. Please give me a call back when you get this message." Click. I put down the phone and rolled over to go to sleep. I checked the time on the clock next to Azera's side of the bed. The time was 3:28 am. I decided to try again to get some sleep and call Dayton back after about 6:00 a.m.

I woke up at 8:00 am. I rolled over and checked my phone to see if Dayton called or texted me. I had no missed calls and only one text message from Azera's father. From Dayton, nothing. I got up, washed up and brushed my teeth. I went downstairs and fed Azera her breakfast. I made myself a cup of coffee. I put the cup to my mouth to take a sip and immediately I felt sick to my stomach. I just knew I was going to throw up. I put my hand across my mouth and grabbed my stomach and ran into the downstairs bathroom. It felt like I was throwing up for hours. Jae'mi walked into the bathroom and asked me if I was ok. "Yeah, I'm ok" I lied. I stood up and Jae'mi helped me walk back into the kitchen. I sat at the kitchen table and tried to figure out what I had eaten the night before.

"Saniya, what did you eat last night? Jae'mi asked.

"Nothing, I haven't been hungry lately. It seemed that everything made me sick to my stomach so I really hadn't been eating much of anything in the last few days.

"Maybe you should eat something Saniya. It's not good to go without eating, especially with the stress you've been under lately." Jae'mi spoke to me, but she still seemed a little annoyed.

"I'll eat later." I replied.

"Have you spoken to Dayton?" Jae'mi asked me, seeming like she already knew the answer.

"No I haven't, he won't answer the phone or call me back." I told Jae'mi.

"Maybe you should just give him some time Saniya." I understood what Jae'mi was saying, I just didn't want him to think I don't care. I excused myself from the table and decided I needed to lay down for a few until the nausea I felt subsided.

I went upstairs and lay across my bed. I picked up my cell phone and dialed Dayton's number. Again I got no answer. I decided not to leave him a message this time. Damn, maybe I really messed things up for myself. Nothing happened between Evan and me but Dayton's not giving me the chance to explain that to him. Frustrated, I lay down and took a nap. While I was sleeping, Azera's father came to get her and take her out for the day.

My phone rang and woke me up. It was Azera calling me to say hi. After she and I talked for a few minutes, I got up and decided to go for a walk to get some air. "Jae'mi, I'm going to go for a walk." I yelled to my sister. "Are you sure you want to go for a walk by yourself Saniya?" I can come with you if you want."
"No, I'm not going to be scared to be alone Jae'mi. I can't let what happened to me keep me from living." I explained, hoping she would understand what I was saying.
"I understand" she said with reservation in her voice. I walked out of the

front door and began to take my walk. I started walking and my phone immediately started ringing. Ring...Ring...Ring... I looked at the caller id and I didn't recognize the number. I answered the phone calmly. "Hello."

"Where are you going beautiful?" It was Sebastian.

"Fuck you!" I yelled into the phone. Then Click, I hung up. I was terrified. How in the hell did he know I left the house? I looked all around me. No cars were going by and there was nobody outside but me. Again, my phone rang and the same number flashed across the screen. I sent it to voicemail. I turned around to head back to the house. I was too afraid to take that walk after all. Again, my phone rang. Same number. I answered it this time. "What in the fuck do you want?" I yelled into the phone.

"Don't hang up Saniya, if you do I'll make another visit to your sister's house and this time I won't be so nice." Sebastian threatened.

"Why are you calling me Sebastian? And why are you following me? Sebastian I'm telling you for the last time, leave me the fuck alone! I don't want you!" I screamed hysterically into the phone.

"Well I want you and I will have you again Saniya, one way or another."

"The only thing you're going to have is a fucking jail cell with your name on it you bastard!"

"Oh I'm going to get that pussy again Saniya, believe that!"

"I'll kill you if you ever come near me again!" I screamed into the phone.

Sebastian just laughed at me. This enraged me!

"You, kill me?" "Ha ha"... Saniya you're funny as hell!" He taunted.

Again, I hung up the phone on Sebastian and continued to head back to the house. Thank God I was only four houses away from our house. I rushed back into the house and straight up to Jae'mi's room. "He won't stop calling me!" I yelled as I searched through Jae'mi's closet for the gun she told me I could use.

"Who?" Jae'mi asked as she finished putting on her uniform for work.

"Sebastian!" I cried out, feeling like I was about to have a nervous breakdown.

"He called you again Saniya?"

"Yes, he was watching me. As soon as I left the house he called my phone."

"Saniya you need to change your cell phone number asap!" She was right; I need to do something for myself. I keep running to her and Dayton for them to save me from Sebastian and Evan and I need to save my dam self. I found the metal box with the 9mm gun in it. I got out my key to the box

213

and opened it. "Saniya, I don't want you to do anything crazy." Jae'mi said sounding very concerned. I saw Jae'mi putting on her uniform. I had forgotten she was going to work tonight until I saw her putting on her uniform. That means I'm going to be home with Azera by myself. Dayton won't answer the phone and Jae'mi is going to work. I became so nervous. What in the hell am I going to do? I thought to myself. It was like Jae'mi read my mind. "Saniya if you want me to call out and stay home with you, I will." Jae'mi said but I knew she really didn't want to do that.

"I can't expect you to protect me forever Jae'mi." I said, though I wish she could.

"You still haven't heard from Dayton?" Jae'mi asked.

"No, he won't answer my phone calls nor has he returned any of my calls or my messages." I replied. Jae'mi had disappointment all over her face. "I thought he would be here with you tonight but Saniya, you having Evan over here for whatever reason probably made Dayton re-think his relationship with you. He's been right here for you since the first day he met you, and you have your ass propped up on the couch talking to Evan at two something in the morning."

"You're right." I said to Jae'mi. I felt so stupid I just put my head down and thought about what Jae'mi was saying to me. "But I didn't do anything with Evan he was just telling me..."

"I don't care what he was saying to you", Jae'mi interrupted. It looked bad Saniya." Again Jae'mi was right; I definitely fucked up with Dayton.

"Ok Saniya, I have to go to work. I'll talk to you in a few. I'll call and check up on you and Azera on my break."

"Ok" I said to my sister. With that Jae'mi left for work, and left me all alone.

Ring..Ring...Ring... my phone rang the second she pulled out of the driveway. 'PRIVATE NUMBER' "Hello" I said into my phone.

"So your sister left for work huh?"

"Go fuck yourself Sebastian!" I yelled into the phone. I got my keys and got into my car and I left the house. Ring... Ring... Ring...my phone rings again. I checked the number it was Azera's father. I completely forgot he was dropping Azera off. "Oh shit Waymon, I'm sorry I had to run out for a minute, can you keep Azera tonight for me please?" "Yeah Saniya, I got you, everything ok?" "You sound upset." Waymon said sounding very concerned.

"I'm cool Waymon, I just had an emergency come up."

"Ok, if you need me, you know I got you Saniya."

"I know Waymon, thank you."

"No problem babe." Waymon still called me babe even though we have been broken up for a few years. I fucked up that relationship too. I was dancing to make money instead of getting a regular job like Waymon suggested I do. He made enough money to support me, him and Azera, but I insisted on having my own money. I was craving all the attention I was getting from the men at the club and I ended up cheating on him. I called out the other man's name while we were making love one night and of course he figured out what was going on and dumped me immediately. I tried everything in my power to get him back, but he just didn't want me anymore. Can't blame him at all after what I did to him.

I headed to Menlo Park Mall to walk around and clear my head. I needed to have a game plan to stop Sebastian from harassing me. Ring... Ring... Ring... 'Private number' "What!" I yelled into the phone. "When are you coming home Saniya? I miss you!" Sebastian said in that sinister voice. "Click" I immediately hung up. I called T-mobile and immediately changed my cell phone number. My next call went to Plainfield Police Department. I reported that Sebastian was calling me and I had a restraining order on him. I also let them know that he was somewhere around the house where I was staying. They told me to stop by the police station so I could make a formal statement. I started to ask if Dayton was at work, but I didn't want to seem like some insecure girlfriend. I hung up with the police department, and got back into my car to head there.

I stopped by the police station and made my complaint. I didn't see Dayton while I was there. The police officer I made the report with informed me that they had been unable to find Sebastian to serve him with the harassment and the restraining order violation warrants they had for him the phone calls and the visit to the house. This meant they still hadn't caught him since he was bailed out. I left the police department so frustrated. I headed straight home to go to bed.

I pulled into the driveway and stepped out of my car. It was eerily quiet on our street. I got my keys out and I unlocked the front door. I walked in and punched in the code to disarm the house alarm. All the lights were out in the house. I was scared but I decided I wasn't going to let Sebastian's bullshit get to me tonight. I headed to the kitchen and got myself a glass of wine. I took the wine and locked all of the doors and checked all of the windows in the house. I set the alarm and then headed upstairs to my sister's room. Since I had the house all to myself, I figured I would relax in her bed and watch some TV on the 40 inch while she was at work. I went into my room and changed into my pajamas... grabbed my phone and called Jae'mi to give her my new cell phone number. We talked briefly and then I called Dayton to give him the new number. I dialed his number and again, no answer. I left him a voice mail. I called Azera's father and gave him my new number. I spoke to Azera and made sure she put the number in her cell phone. A few hours went by and I still didn't hear anything from Dayton and I began to get a really tired. The time on the clock read 12:34 am. I tried one more time to call Dayton and he finally answered the phone. "Hi Dayton, its Saniya. Did you get the messages I left for you?"

"No, I haven't checked my voicemail." he replied dryly. "I'm still at work and it was a busy day today."

"Oh ok, I'm sorry" I said suddenly feeling like I was imposing.

"It's cool Saniya." He said, again not sounding too enthusiastic about my call.

"Dayton, I just want to say I'm really sorry about what happened last night."

"Saniya I don't want to talk about that." He interrupted. Damn, he just shut me up quick. I thought to myself "Ok Dayton." I said. Awkward silence. "How's Serenity doing today?" I asked trying to ease some of the tension between us. His voice lightened up a little.

"She's good, I checked on her earlier."

"Oh ok cool." More awkward silence. "Ok Dayton, umm I guess I'll let you go."

"Ok Saniya, I'll talk to you in a few, I should be getting off in about an hour or so. I'll give you a call when I get home." His voice sounded a little more cheerful.

"Ok Dayton, I'll talk to you in a few."

"Bye Dayton,"

"Bye Saniya."

Click.

At least I got to speak to him tonight I thought to myself. I know he's not going to call me back. I watched about 20 minutes of TV and then I thought I heard something downstairs, but I shrugged it off as me being paranoid. I did mute the TV to see if I heard anything else. I heard nothing. I un-muted the TV and rolled over to finish watching 'The Wendy

Williams Show' on BET. I ran into the room and got my sleeping pills to get one to help me fall to sleep. I took one and swallowed it with my last sip of wine. I flipped through a couple of shows Jae'mi had dvr'd until I got to 'Bridezillas'. I decided to watch that until I drifted off to sleep.

I was dreaming that Dayton was rubbing my back and kissing me on my neck. I was moaning and kissing him back in my dream until I realized that I wasn't dreaming, someone was kissing me and rubbing my breasts under my pajama top. I opened my eyes and stared straight into Sebastian's face. "What in the fuck." I tried to yell, but it only came out as a whisper. He had his hand around my neck and I could hardly talk. I tried to kick my legs up but they had been duck taped together so when I kicked I could only kick straight up. I tried to bend my knees, but they had also been taped together. "Hey beautiful." Sebastian whispered in my ear. "Fuck you" I said as loud as I could.
"Oh that's exactly what I plan to do baby... I'm going to fuck the shit out of you!" Sebastian said then took one of my breasts in his mouth. I squirmed and kicked and tried to bring my hands down to push his head away from my breast. That's when I realized he had taped my hands together. "You can't remember how good I fucked you before, but you'll remember how

220

good I fuck you this time!" He taunted.

"No!" I finally yelled out as loud as I could. Sebastian took his hand from around my neck, and I was finally able to yell like I wanted to. "Yeah Saniya, scream baby!" "I want you to fight it, I like that shit!" Sebastian yelled into my ear. "This good pussy you got, I'm going to be in it all night!" he said.

"You fucking piece of shit!" I yelled.

"Say another word and I'll stick my dick down your fucking throat!" he threatened.

"Yeah, and I'll bite that shit off you bastard!" Sebastian flipped me over on my stomach and pulled my pants down to my knees. "Look at all that beautiful ass!" Sebastian said and then kissed me on my ass. I tried like hell to flip back over onto my back, but Sebastian had straddled me and was sitting on my legs. He stuck his tongue in my ass and began to lick me. I screamed for him to stop, but he just kept licking me and then he stuck his fingers inside of me. I kicked and screamed for him to stop but he wouldn't. "I'm getting ready to tear that pussy up!" He said as he laughed at me. I heard him unbuckling his belt and then I assumed he was pulling down his pants. He lifted up my ass and rammed his dick into me. I screamed as loud as I could scream. "NO!"

221

"Yes Saniya, take this good dick!" He said in that crazy man's voice. He fucked me like I was some kind of dog. I screamed for someone to help me. "Yeah baby scream, I love it when you scream, it makes my dick even harder.

"You little dick bastard! I yelled at Sebastian. He rammed himself deeper inside of me.

"Take this dick Saniya!" he yelled back. He pulled himself out of me and flipped me over onto my back. "No!" I screamed out as loud as I could then BAM! I heard a loud bang, and Sebastian's body fell off to the side and off of the bed.

"Saniya, are you ok?" I heard his voice, but I couldn't believe it.

"Dayton?"

"Yes, it's me baby!" he yelled to me.

"Oh God! Thank you God, thank you!!" I cried. Dayton ran over to me and with a knife he cut the tape that bound my hands and my knees. I scrambled off of the bed and onto the floor on the other side of the bed.

"Did he hurt you Saniya?"

"Yes!" I cried out. "Is he dead?" I asked tears streaming down my face. "A female officer walked over to Sebastian and checked his pulse.

"No pulse Dayton." she said as she shook her head.

222

"Ok." he responded. Suddenly I noticed there were cops everywhere.

"Give me the gun Saniya." Dayton said the words, but they didn't register in my head at first.

"What Dayton?" I asked totally confused

"Saniya, give me the gun baby." I looked down and there was the 9mm Jae'mi had hidden in her closet in my hands. I handed the gun over to Dayton, and then I fell into his arms.

"Saniya, where did you get this gun from?" Dayton asked me.

"Huh?" "Where did you get this gun from Saniya?"

"Jae'mi's closet" I cried.

After the paramedics checked to see if Sebastian had any signs of life, they came over to check me out. I just couldn't seem to let go of Dayton. He pleaded with me to let the paramedics check me out, but I couldn't let them touch me. I didn't want anyone to touch me other than Dayton. I just laid there half in his arms and half on the floor, sobbing uncontrollably. Finally I agreed to go to the hospital but only if Dayton agreed to come with me.

The Sum of My Mistakes

Chapter Thirty-One

Dayton

"Give me the gun." I told Saniya. She was in such shock she hesitated for a minute. She finally gave me the gun and fell into my arms. She sobbed uncontrollably while I held her. My partner Ky checked to see if Sebastian had a pulse. She didn't feel one. I asked Saniya where she got the gun from. She pointed and told me she got it from Jae'mi's closet. The rescue squad and paramedics came in and started working on Sebastian. One of the squad members walked over to check Saniya out, but she wouldn't let him touch her. She just held on to me and continued to cry. There were fellow officers everywhere. They all looked at me sort of awkward. My Sgt. Got a sheet and covered Saniya up. She asked Saniya again to please let the squad check her out and take her to the hospital. Saniya finally agreed to go to the hospital to get checked out. She only agreed to go if I went with her to the hospital. My sergeant said it was fine so I agreed to go. I helped the paramedics cover Saniya up and load her into the ambulance. In the ambulance I called Jae'mi and told her what happened. She couldn't believe what I was telling her. Hell I couldn't believe what was happening. Sebastian actually got into the house and raped Saniya again. It messed me up when I walked upstairs and saw him raping her. I was about to blow his head off when Saniya shot him. I didn't even get the chance to cock my weapon when I heard the shot go off. Thank God Jae'mi had that gun in the house.

The ride in the ambulance was somber and quiet. Saniya was still crying but she was finally calming down. We had to take her to Robert Wood Johnson's Hospital so we had a little bit of a ride. She wouldn't let go of me during the entire trip. . Sebastian miraculously had a pulse when the paramedics got to the scene so they were flying him out to UMDNJ trauma center in Newark.

"Saniya, are you ok?" I asked her hoping she was finally calming down a little.

 "I don't know Dayton." She responded. It was obvious that she was completely traumatized.

We arrived at the hospital and they took her into one of the trauma rooms. I didn't know whether to follow her into the room or sit out in the lobby. I've never been put into a situation like this before. I didn't know what to feel. I know I'd only been around Saniya for a short time and I've watched her go through hell. I'll be honest, I don't know whether to stay or go right now.

Half hour later the doctor came out of Saniya's room and walked straight up to me. "Officer Long?" She asked.

"Yes doctor?" I immediately stood up to greet the doctor.

"Ms. Wheeler is asking for you, can you follow me please." I did as the doctor asked and followed her into the room where I saw them take Saniya. I walked in and saw her lying in that bed, hooked up to the oxygen tank, with an IV hanging out of her arm. The doctor told me they had her on some type of sedative. She was sedate and resting quietly. I walked up to the bed. Sanyia opened her eyes and said my name. "Dayton."

"Yes Saniya?" I responded back.

"I'm sorry." She whispered.

"Why are you apologizing to me Saniya?"

"Because I really want to be with you, but now I can't."

I was confused by what she just said to me. "Saniya, it's the medication messing with you. Don't think about that right now."

"No Dayton, I have to tell you this!" Saniya began to get upset and cry again. I watched the tears fall from her eyes and down her face and wondered what was making her so upset.

"Ok Saniya, why can't you be with me?" I asked trying to calm her down a little.

"Saniya, are you ok?" SJae'mi busted into Saniya's hospital door and ran up to her. Oh my God Saniya, you're all bruised up." Jae'mi said beginning to get upset herself. "Hi Dayton, I'm so sorry I didn't speak." Jae'mi said as she came around to the side of the bed where I was standing and gave me a hug.

"It's ok Jae'mi, I understand." I said as I hugged her back.

Jae'mi kissed Saniya on her cheek and sat in the chair next to her bed. They must have given her something very strong, because Saniya began to drift off to sleep. The doctor came back into the room and asked if she could see me out in the hallway. "Of course doctor." I said. I turned to

Jae'mi and told her I'd be back in a few minutes. As I walked out of Saniya's hospital room door, My partner Ky Davies was walking towards us along with a few more of my fellow officers. "Hey Dayton" my partner said to me as she approached Dr. Davis and I.

"Hey Ky." I said back.

"How's Saniya doing?" She asked Dr. Davis and I. Dr. Davis answered her question speaking to the both of us. "She's ok physically considering what's happened to her. It's her mental state that I'm worried about, that's what I wanted to talk to you about Officer Long."

"What's up Dr. Davis?"

"We're going to keep Saniya here for a few days. She's bruised pretty badly physically and she seems to be severely depressed and traumatized. I'm afraid she may be suffering from Post-Traumatic Stress Syndrome and I want to bring in our social worker to talk to her.

"I agree Dr. Davis she really should talk to someone.

The other officers still need to question Saniya and find out what went on before we got to the scene. I will go in and tell her sister what's going on." My partner Ky, my supervisor, Sgt. Meyers and I went into Saniya's room to question her about what happened prior to our arrival. To the house I had to take off my friend hat, put my police hat back on and do my job. All that kept flashing back to me was how brutal Sebastian was with Saniya. It was only for a few seconds as we walked into the room, but that memory will stick with me forever.

Ky must have sensed that I was too emotionally involved with this situation so she jumped right in and started the questioning. Saniya couldn't recall everything that happened, but she did tell us that she was sleeping and suddenly felt someone feeling her breasts. She said she opened her eyes and there was Sebastian holding her down and touching her. She told us how she screamed for him to leave her alone but he just wouldn't stop. He told her he was going to tear her ass up. She was crying while she told us the horrible story. She said she put the gun under the pillow before she went to sleep, but she couldn't recall when she actually picked it up from under the pillow and fired. She explained to us that she tried to call me a few times, before the incident to let me know she was going to be home alone, but got no response at first. She recalled how I was short with her when she called. Immediately I felt guilty as hell. I was so upset about seeing Evan there; I didn't want to answer the phone when she called. When I did talk to her, I kept it brief and hung up as soon as I could.

We all listened to her story and my Sgt. decided to advise the prosecutor not to press charges against Saniya for having that gun. It was clearly self-defense and she was in the confines of her home. The gun was registered to Jae'mi, she had previously been attacked by Sebastian, and she felt threatened that's why she utilized the gun in the first place.

My Sgt.'s cell phone rang and she walked out of the room to take the call. I felt so guilty for not being there for Saniya, I could hardly face her. I decided to go out into the lobby and wait for my fellow officers to finish talking to Saniya.

I headed for the door and Jae'mi asked "Dayton, where are you going?" "Nowhere just out in the lobby." I responded.
I looked back at Saniya and she didn't try to stop me from going. So I left. I couldn't handle what was going on with her. I don't know what was happening with me, but I had this overwhelming feeling of guilt. I should have been there. I should have been with her. I should have answered my phone earlier when she was trying to call me, so I would know she was

going to be alone last night. All types of thoughts ran through my head. I knew I had to put those feelings aside and do my job, but for some reason I just couldn't.

After about 15 minutes I was getting ready to go back into the room and my Sgt. walked over to me and gave me some unbelievable news. "Dayton, Sebastian Young is still alive."

"What?" Sarge? No you have to be kidding me!" I said completely taken aback by the news.

"Yes, he's in seriously critical condition, but it seems that they got him to surgery just in time."

"No!" I said much to my sergeant's surprise. I had never wanted someone dead before, but after what I saw him do to Saniya, I will be honest, I wanted him to die. "Sarge, how am I going to tell Saniya this?"

"I don't know Dayton, but you can't keep it from her." my Sergeant replied. She was right; I needed to tell Saniya and Jae'mi what was happening. I walked back into Saniya's hospital room and broke the news to everyone in there.

"Saniya, I don't want you to be worried, but so far, Sebastian didn't die from his injuries. He's still in surgery and he's still in pretty critical condition."

"NO!" Saniya screamed. "Please God no!"

The Sum of My Mistakes

Chapter Thirty-Two

Macy

Damn it's been three days and no sign of Sebastian. I just knew once he

got my letter he would come and get me out. I called that stupid ass Renee

and she told me she delivered the letter to Sebastian's grandmother. I told

that dumb bitch not to give it to anyone else other than Sebastian. I pray

that old lady doesn't open that letter. I would hate to have to go kill

her old ass because of Renee's dumb ass.

Well I'm going to court tomorrow morning. I guess I'll have to do these 30

days since I can't seem to get the money up to get the hell out of here. I

don't know why in the hell I thought Sebastian's ass would come and bail

me out. He's just another worthless negro.

My new cellmate came in today. I wish I could just have this cell all to myself. I don't need another dumb bitch Like Renee in here with me although my new roommate was a good looking female with a pretty face and long beautiful brown hair. She looked like she could have been a model back in the day. She was medium build with big breasts and a big ass. I don't like pretty girls. They always thought they were the shit. I'm not a pretty girl, I'm fucking beautiful. I've always been beautiful with a sexy little body and a sassy little haircut. Of course I've been looking a little rough since I've been in here but once I get back home, if I still have an apartment I can get to my makeup and my flat iron. Then I can look like my normal self.

My cellmate came into our cell and put her things down on the floor. "Hi" she said to me dryly, never even looking at me. She just threw her linens up on her bunk and began to make it up. "Whatever" I said back to her. She completely ignored me. I sat up in my bunk and picked up the book I was reading... The Choir Director by Carl Weber. I noticed my cellmate's newspaper sitting on the floor and I reached down to pick it up and read it. "Don't touch my shit!" She yelled at me as she snatched the paper out of my hand.

"Damn I was just looking at it!" I yelled back.

"I don't give a shit what you were looking at bitch, don't touch my shit!"

She snapped again. She looked like she was going to kill me. I started to

snap on her but; instead I just lay back down on my bunk and ignored her

ignorant ass. I was angry as hell that she yelled at me but I can't get in any

trouble while I'm in here. My court date is tomorrow and I'm not trying to

get any extra time added on to my 30 days. I guess my attitude when she

tried to say hi didn't help so I'll just stay away from her ass.

It was dinner time and I was starving. My new cellmate left our cell a

while ago and left her newspaper still sitting on the floor. I picked it up

and read the story that was on the front cover. Former Stripper shoots

Personal trainer. No charges filed. I immediately scrolled down to the

article. 'Saniya Wheeler who filed sexual battery charges against shooting

victim Sebastian Young prior to this incident will not be charged with any

crimes related to the shooting. Sebastian Young is in grave condition

at UMDNJ hospital in Newark.' I read the rest of the article and it said that

Sebastian broke into Saniya's house and raped her for the second time

within the last week. He was just released from jail on a $50,000 bail for

his arrest in the drugging and possible sexual battery of Saniya. "I just

don't believe this shit." I said out loud. I was completely disgusted. Why would he want to sexually assault her ugly fat ass? I wondered. This article can't be true. I threw the paper back down onto the floor and lay back down on the bed. I felt sick to my stomach and I wanted to throw up. I balled up into the fetal position and just cried. "What in the hell am I going to do?" I cried out loud. I knew no one was going to care whether I was crying or not. I didn't give a shit how much noise I was making. My plan will never come to fruition. I'll never have Evan all to myself. All because of that fucking Saniya! She fucked up everything!

My cellmate returned from wherever she was. She walked in and asked me was I ok. "You aiight?" she said as she climbed up onto her bunk. "Yeah, I'm alright." I said back to her. I decided to not be nasty this time and just answer her.

"You need to talk about it?" She asked.

"No." I responded.

"Ok." She said finishing the conversation.

I finally stopped crying and eventually I drifted off to sleep. I woke up to the guards announcing lights out. "Damn I slept through dinner." I said out loud. My cellmate heard me and asked me if I wanted an apple. At first I was going to say no, but then I realized I had to eat. "Sure" I said as nicely as I could. She got up and climbed down off her bunk. She pulled out an apple from under her shirt she had folded on the little table by our beds. "Here you go." She said as she handed the apple to me.

"Thanks." I said to her.

"Name's Lana, Lana King." She said as she sat down next to me on my bunk.

"Macy, Macy Long." I introduced myself.

"Good to meet you Macy."

"Likewise." I said as I bit into the apple she gave me.

"I'm not trying to get in your business Macy, but you alright?" Lana asked me again.

"I just found out a good friend of mine was shot and is not doing too good." I told Lana.

"Oh that guy in the newspaper that got shot was a friend of yours?"

"Yes, I'm pregnant and he's the father of my baby." I confessed to Lana. I can't believe I just told Lana that. I thought to myself. For some reason I felt comfortable with her.

"Dam Macy, that's fucked up!" Lana said sounding really shocked to hear what I was telling her. I was equally shocked that I was being so honest with her. I told Lana about my relationship with Sebastian and my love for Evan. She sat there and listened to my every word. She was supportive and kind and not judgmental. We stayed up half the night just talking. We finally fell asleep and woke up when it was time to eat breakfast.

Lana was dressed and ready to go when I woke up. I was staring having missed dinner last night. "Morning Macy." Lana said smiling at me. "Good morning Lana." I said back returning the smile. I hurried up and got dressed so that I can go to breakfast with her. We decided to sit together and talk a little more. I don't know why but I felt something for Lana. I usually don't fuck with pretty females. They don't like me because they know I look better than them. They always want to give me a dam attitude.

It was court day for me; I got myself prepared to see the judge. Hopefully they will let me out of this hell hole. I walked into the court room and sat with the rest of the inmates. I tried to keep myself calm and not get smart with the judge.

The clerk called my name and I went up to the defendant's table and stood next to my public defender. I figured they were going to just bring up all of the tickets that got me here, but that wasn't the case. The reason why they brought me back to the county was because I hadn't honored the terms of my release the last time I was here. I was supposed to come up with $1,564 by the end of the day or they would re-issue the warrant for my arrest. I never came up with the money so my bail wasn't just the $3,000 for the traffic warrants, it was the $3,000 plus the child support warrant. I was never going to get the hell out of here. The judge asked me if I had any of the child support money. Of course I didn't so I just simply said no. Then I found out that every violation that I had in every city I was pulled over or had a parking ticket I would have to pay for before I would be released. That means, I could pay off 1 ticket in one city, but I still wouldn't be released until I paid them all. I was so screwed. I was about to get my bail amount and go sit back down until I was taken back to my cell, but the officer on the computer in the courtroom then ended up giving me the surprise of my life. "Judge Coleman, Mrs. Long has another warrant for her arrest in South Plainfield your honor, just issued this morning."

"What is that warrant for Officer Culpepper?"

"Attempted Murder Your Honor."

My public defender looked at me like I was crazy.

Instantly I knew Sebastian's grandmother read the letter. All I could do was scream. "No!"

The Sum of My Mistakes

Chapter Thirty-Three

Evan

I woke up in my hospital room. I'd forgotten where I was for a minute. I looked over to my right and saw Ethan lying in the bed next to me. Heaven was sitting in the chair in between us sleeping.

Dr. Holmes came into the room and said hello. Heaven immediately woke up. Dr. Holmes began to examine Ethan. Heaven finally realized I was awake and came over to my bed to say good morning. "Hi Uncle Evan." Heaven said smiling all over.

"Good morning Heaven." I responded still feeling a little groggy.

"Good morning Evan." Dr. Holmes said as he came over to examine me.

"Morning Dr. Holmes." I spoke back. "How's Ethan doing doctor?" I asked. I was so worried about my brother. I wasn't even thinking about myself.

"He's doing better than he was yesterday." Dr. Holmes said seeming relieved that I finally woke up.

"How are you feeling Evan?" Dr. Holmes asked me as he helped me sit up so he could listen to my lungs.

"I'm ok doc." I told him.

After my blood type was tested yesterday, Dr. Holmes rushed to examine me to see if I was healthy enough for surgery. Thank God I take care of myself. The blood test results came in and I was in a hospital gown, signing a release form and laying down on an operating table counting from 10 backwards within minutes of coming up a match for Ethan's blood type. The rest is a big blur.

Dr. Holmes was done examining me and Heaven and I were talking when I heard his voice. "Good morning." Big Evan said, interrupting our conversation. "Grand-pop!" Heaven squealed then jumped up and ran to greet Big Evan.

"Hello My love." Big Evan said to Heaven. They hugged for a few seconds and then broke their embrace.

"Grand-pop you're back!" Heaven said to Big Evan. "Yes I am baby, how's your dad?" Big Evan asked Heaven as he looked over at Ethan lying in the bed next to mine. "Hello Evan." He said to me as he searched my face for a reaction to him speaking to me. I didn't give him one.

"Good morning Big Evan." I calmly said to my father. I couldn't believe that I actually spoke to him. I was still upset with him and the way he has treated me over the years, but after what he told me about the situation with my mother I just see him so differently now.

Big Evan took a seat next to Ethan's bed on the other side of the room. I could tell he was still feeling a little apprehensive about conversing with me. After seeing Ethan, I could not understand how in the hell he had any doubt that I was his son. I began thinking about the bad times between us and began to feel angry all over again. I wanted to say what I was feeling but I didn't want to bring that anger to Ethan and Heaven. So I just sat there quiet. I decided when I felt a little stronger that I would get a DNA test done for Big Evan and myself. If nothing more, I wanted to prove to this man that I was his son. Once that was done, I'd have the pleasure of watching the guilt eat him alive.

Big Ethan sat next to Ethan's bed like a mother bear protecting her cub. I was secretly jealous, but didn't say a word. I lay quietly on my bed, as Heaven sat on the side of the bed talking to me about all the wonderful things she wanted Ethan and I to do once he got better and out of the hospital. I loved her enthusiasm; I just didn't know how interested Ethan would be in having a relationship with me. God only knows what big Evan has told him about me.

Ethan began to wake up. He was still pretty groggy but he called out Heaven's name and everyone directed their attention to him. "Heaven, is Evan ok?" Ethan asked before he turned his head to the left to see me. "Yes Ethan, I'm fine." I answered him.

Heaven climbed off of my bed and walked over to Ethan's bed. "Hi daddy, how are you feeling?" Heaven asked Ethan.

"I'm good baby, I feel way better than I've felt in a long time." he responded. "Hi dad" he said to Big Evan. Not in the loving and caring way I thought he would, but in a way that had me curious as to what was really going on between them. Ethan seemed annoyed with Big Evan. Big Evan's reaction to Ethan struck me as kind of odd also. He was very stand-off-ish, very quiet and seemed almost as the child instead of the parent. "Hi

Ethan." Big Evan responded and that was it. No more words were exchanged between the two of them. Big Evan just sat there and awkwardly stared at Ethan and Heaven as they talked. They included me in their banter, but I was so fixated on Big Evan and Ethan ignoring each other, that I was barely speaking.

Ethan's mother showed up after about an hour of Big Evan getting there. "Ethan" his mother said as she stepped into the room.

"Mom!" Ethan said with a big smile on his face. "How are you mom?" he asked her as she bent over to kiss him on the cheek.

"Hi Me-Mah" Heaven said to her grandmother.

"My Heaven!" Ethan's mother responded. The two ladies embraced each other and gave each other a peck on the cheek. Big Evan and Ethan's mom never spoke. They didn't even acknowledge one another.

My cell phone rang and a strange number popped up on my screen. I started not to answer my phone, but I had a feeling it was something important. It was Tia, Asia's sister. The one who was taking care of the kids for me. "Hi Evan, its Tia. The kids want to speak to you."

"Thanks Tia" I said as she put Isis on the phone first. "Hi daddy." Isis said sounding like she really actually wanted to talk to me for once. "Hey sweetheart" I replied. Isis went on talking to me like we spoke every day. She seemed to enjoy talking to me and told me everything that has happened in her life since I left them two days ago. She then handed the phone over to her brother who was a little short in conversation, but he did ask me a bunch of questions about my trip and his uncle Ethan. I humored both kids and although I was still feeling a little groggy, it was nice talking to my kids. Even Tia got on the phone and gave me an update on Asia's progress. Things were getting a little better and she seemed to be improving slightly. The doctors even downgraded her from grave condition to critical condition. In the grand scheme of things, that's definitely a better prognosis. Seriously, I didn't think Asia was going to make it out of this alive.

I was about to hang up and Tia hit me with some huge news. She read in the newspaper and saw on the news that Sebastian had raped Saniya and she had shot him in self-defense. At first when she told me the news about him raping her, I was a bit confused. I thought she was referring to the incident that happened before I left. Then she told me he had broken into Jae'mi's house when no one was there but Saniya and brutally raped her again. My blood began to boil. I became so infuriated I had to abruptly hang up. Heaven saw it in my eyes and asked me what was wrong. I couldn't even talk. I began to sweat profusely and felt a terrible pain in my chest and down my left arm. I felt dizzy and I thought I was going to throw up. I truly thought I was going to die. Heaven ran to the door and screamed for a doctor, Big Evan and his wife rushed to my side. I tried to speak but I couldn't say a word. So many things flashed in my mind and I thought about all of the things Heaven and I were just talking about me doing with Ethan when we both got out of here. I thought about Saniya and Azera and all of the fucked up things I did to Saniya. My entire life flashed before my eyes. Next thing I knew everything went black.

The Sum of My Mistakes

Chapter Thirty-Four

Saniya

I opened my eyes and saw Jae'mi sleeping at the foot of my bed. Dayton was in the chair knocked out also and Waymon was leaning against the wall by the door.

"Jae'mi." I called to my sister to wake her up. She raised her head and smiled at me. I tried to smile back but I just couldn't. I was feeling too horrible. My entire body was sore and I felt sick to my stomach. Waymon walked over and tapped Dayton on his shoulder to tell him that I was awake. Dayton looked over at me and Jae'mi and said "Good morning ladies." He then looked at Waymon and said "What's up man?" Thanks for waking me up. Waymon said you're welcome and then he walked over to my bed and touched me on my foot. "Saniya, how are you feeling?" he asked.

"Horrible." I responded. I was shocked to see that Waymon was there.

We've gone through some serious changes but he always had my back.

Dayton got up from the chair and walked over to me, he looked tired.

"Hey baby, how are you?" Dayton said to me smiling.

"Hi Dayton." I said attempting to smile back at him. The smile just wouldn't come.

"Saniya do you have to go the bathroom or are you hungry or anything?" Jae'mi asked me.

"Yes, I do have to go to the bathroom."

"Ok, do you need help standing up?" Dayton asked.

"Yes please." I said to Dayton.

Dayton put the side rail down on the bed and took my hand to help me up out of the bed. I stood up and I immediately got dizzy. Almost every part of my body was aching. I eased back down onto the bed and sat there for a minute. Suddenly I felt even sicker to my stomach. I tried to get myself together, but I just knew I was going to throw up. Dayton must have seen the look on my face, because he immediately grabbed the garbage can and placed it right in front of me. You would have thought I was throwing my life up into that can. I finished vomiting and I felt so weak. Although I had to go to the bathroom I didn't think I would make it there. Dayton

249

helped me lay back down on the bed and Waymon looked at me suspiciously. I immediately remembered what the doctor told me right before Dayton came into my room last night. He told me a pregnancy test they took on me came out positive. I was just about to tell Dayton I couldn't see him anymore because I was pregnant when Jae'mi busted in the room. Now I was positive Waymon figured out that I was pregnant and I wouldn't be able to keep this a secret for very long. Only thing is I was never late for my period and I had no symptoms prior to a few days ago. When I was pregnant with Azera it was the same thing, I knew almost immediately. The second or third day I was pregnant I was throwing up and sick like this. Oh my God. What am I going to do now?

"Saniya are you ok?" Dayton and Jae'mi both asked me at the same time. Waymon just sat there staring at me.
"I'll be ok." I said to Jae'mi and Dayton. I was about to attempt to go to the bathroom again when the nurse walked in the door. "How are we feeling today dear?" the nurse asked me.
"I'm not feeling too good." I said to the nurse. "Well you've been through an extremely traumatic experience young lady and you're not going to feel like your old self for a while. I looked around at Dayton, Jae'mi and

Waymon and hoped and prayed that this nurse wouldn't mention anything about the baby. "I need to take you to the bathroom and the doctor needs to examine you, so I need for all of you to step out for a minute please. The nurse said to the three of them. Oh thank God she didn't say anything to them about the baby, I thought to myself.

One by one Dayton, Jae'mi and Waymon all quietly walked out of my room. Waymon was the last one to leave. He stopped, looked at me for a moment and then left out the door. Never saying a word. I knew that this would be Waymon and my little secret.

The nurse walked over to me and said she needed to take my blood pressure. I stuck out my left arm and she put the blood pressure cuff around my arm and began to press on the little bulb to inflate the cuff. "Thank you." I said to the nurse as the blood pressure cuff began to get tight around my arm. "You're welcome." was all she said back to me. At that moment, the doctor walked in the door and asked me how I was feeling. I went through the same routine with him as I did the nurse a few minutes earlier. Ms. Wheeler, I would like to release you today, but I just need for you to speak with our social worker before you are discharged." "Ok doctor." I said not really wanting to but agreeing to anyway if it meant I could get the hell out of this hospital. The doctor did a small examination on me and asked me a few questions about my last period. I told the doctor about my previous pregnancy and recommended I get to a private doctor or the clinic as soon as possible. Especially if I'm not going to keep the baby. That thought had entered my mind and I was already going to look for places to have it done. I promised myself I would never get rid of a child, but under these circumstances, I think I'll have to go back on that promise. The doctor and the nurse both turned to walk out of my room when the social worker walked in. We had a brief chat and although I never had any intentions on doing so, I agreed to speak to a psychiatrist or psychologist as soon as I got settled in at home. I played the part of sane while the social worker and everyone else were there. Deep down, I was about to have a nervous breakdown. I went through all of the motions like I was ok. Jae'mi and Dayton came back into the room, but Jae'mi said that Waymon went home to check on Azera and to get her ready to come see me. I explained to them that I will be going home and that someone needed to call Waymon and tell him to bring Azera there. Jae'mi did so and Dayton began to help me try and stand up again so I could put on the clothes Jae'mi had run to the house and gotten me to wear home. I was able to stand this time and with help from Dayton I was able to get dressed. I finished getting dressed and I lay back on the bed for a while until the nurse came back into my room and officially discharged me. She had me sign my release forms and gave me paperwork for everything we discussed. She never said a word about the pregnancy and Thank God because Dayton and Jae'mi were hanging on her every word for what to do when we all got home. Dayton was helping me get up from the bed while Jae'mi left to pull her car around. I was reaching for the door to balance myself when I dropped the paper work the nurse had given me. I tried to pick it up myself when Dayton insisted that I let him do it. I squatted down anyway to try and pick the papers up but it was too late. Dayton saw the papers I was praying he wouldn't see. He quickly snatched the papers up from the floor and read them. He looked at me confused and in shock and then with hurt in his eyes he asks "Saniya are you pregnant?"

The Sum of My Mistakes

Chapter Thirty-Five

Dayton

"Saniya, are you pregnant?" I asked her again. She still stood there, frozen with a blank look on her face. Her lack of response told it all. She was pregnant. "Why didn't you say anything Saniya?" Why didn't you tell me?" I asked her. Still no response. "Saniya, say something!" yelled. I didn't expect my voice to get so loud, but I guess my emotions just got the best of me. "I'm sorry Dayton." Was all she could say. "I'm so sorry." she repeated. Then she sat on the floor and sobbed. I just stood there, unable to do anything. How much more can a person take? I thought to myself.

I finally got myself together and I walked over to Saniya and helped her stand up. She was a complete mess. I got some tissue and wiped her face. "Dayton, please don't be mad at me. I tried to tell you yesterday, but Jae'mi walked in and I didn't want her to know. I didn't have an opportunity to tell you again. I'm so sorry!"

"Saniya, it's ok, we'll keep this between the two of us, and we'll figure it all out together."

"Are you serious?" Saniya stopped crying and looked at me shocked.

"Yes, I am. Whatever you want to do I'm cool with it." I reassured her.

"Oh my God! Thank you Dayton!" Saniya yelled.

"No need to thank me Saniya, you know I'm here for you." I said the words, but I wasn't sure if I even believed them anymore. Everything had become so overwhelming.

I held Saniya for a few more seconds and then I told her let's go so we can get her home. I knew Jae'mi would be looking for us soon if we didn't hurry up and get out of that hospital. "Saniya, we do need to tell your sister what's going on with the baby. I can understand you not wanting Evan to know right now, but you can't live with your sister and keep this information away from her." Saniya agreed with me and we headed towards the exit of the hospital.

I saw my Sergeant Sgt. Meyers walking into the hospital and something told me she was coming to talk to me about Sebastian. "Hey Sgt. Meyers how are you?"

"I'm good Dayton, how are you feeling Ms. Wheeler?"

"I'm ok", Saniya said weakly.

"Dayton may I speak to you privately please."

"Sure Sgt. Meyers, I just need to help Saniya into the car and I'll be right with you."

"No problem Dayton." Sgt. Meyers said and then stood off to the side. I helped Saniya into Jae'mi's car and told them I would be to their house in about an hour. The two of them pulled off and I went to go talk to Sgt. Meyers. "Dayton, I just wanted to let you know that Sebastian Long passed away about 20 minutes ago."

"Oh thank God!" I said to Sgt. Meyers. Again, she was shocked by my elation.

"Dayton, are you sure about dealing with this young lady?" Sgt. Meyers caught me off guard with that question. She's not one to get into my business.

"Yeah Sarge why?"

"I'm just making sure you know what' you're getting yourself into Dayton."

"I'm good, Sarge. I know you're only asking me that because of all this crazy shit that's been happening to her, but I'm good." I tried to reassure my Sgt. although honestly I didn't believe it myself.

"As long as you're good." Sgt. Meyers said not looking like she really believed me.

"Look Dayton, I'm not one to get into your business, but this young lady has a lot going on with her. She's been sexually assaulted twice in a week. On top of that, she just killed a man. She seems to be living under a black cloud

"Really, I'm good Sarge." I lied again.

I cut our conversation real short and told my supervisor I needed to get home. I really didn't want to talk about this anymore. I didn't want her to read the concern and reluctance in my face or my voice.

Sgt. Meyers and I walked to our cars and said our goodbyes. I headed home to check on Serenity.

I went by my mom's house to check on Serenity before I went to Saniya's house. I got home and my mother was very upset. "Dayton, we need to talk." My mom said to me as I walked in the door.

"Absolutely mom, what's up?"

"Dayton, Macy keeps calling here looking for you."

"Calling here?" I asked. I was confused.

"Yes calling here." My mother snapped.

"I don't understand that, she knows my cell number."

"Well, I think she's up to something, so be careful."

"I will mommy, thank you. I also want to say thank you for helping me out so much with Serenity."

"You know you're welcome." But Dayton, you're new friend, is she that young lady who shot her personal trainer? I read that in the newspaper and saw it on the news."

"Yeah mom, that's her."

"Dayton, that girl has been through some stuff in her life from what all of the news reports say. You need to be careful; you don't want another Macy on your hands."

"Believe me mom, I'm not trying to go there, I just want to help her get through this very difficult time."

"Ok Dayton, but I know you, I've never seen you so into another person and so quickly."

"I know mommy, but I'm being careful, I promise, this won't be another Macy situation."

"Ok Dayton." My mom finished our conversation. I know she doesn't believe me, but I'm not going through what I went through with Macy with Saniya, I'm not having it. I know Saniya is a good woman, and I know this bullshit that she's been going through is not her fault.

I picked up my little girl to give her some kisses and my cell phone rang. I looked at the number on the screen and was shocked. Why was Evan calling me? "Hello." I said cautiously into the phone.

"Hello, May I speak to Dayton Long please." A female voice asked.

"Speaking." I said

"Mr. Long, My name is Heaven Roberts; I'm Evan Roberts' niece."

"Yes Ms. Roberts, how may I help you?"

"I'm looking for Saniya Wheeler, my Uncle is very sick and he's asking for her."

"May I ask what's wrong with him please?"

"He had a heart attack." Heaven said.

"Wow!" I said into the phone. "Is he ok?"

"So far he's still alive." Heaven said. She didn't sound like his prognosis was very promising.

"Heaven, did you try calling her number?" I asked wondering if she was still ignoring his calls.

"Yes, but I continue to get her voicemail."

"Ok, I'll call her and give you a call back on this phone number, is that ok?"

"Yeah, umm, sure." Heaven said not sounding really convinced.

"Ok, Heaven, I'll give you a call right back."

"Ok, bye."

"Bye."

Click.

I immediately hung up and called Saniya's phone number, and I got her voicemail. I hung up and called Jae'mi's phone number. She picked up on the first ring. "Hey Dayton." Jae'mi said.

"Hey Jae'mi, how are you?"

"I'm good Dayton, how are you?"

"I'm good, may I speak to Saniya please, I tried calling her phone but it keeps taking me to voicemail."

"Sure, absolutely. How's Serenity doing?"

"She's doing fine, sitting up here laughing at me."

"Aww... Dayton, Saniya is in the shower, can I have her call you back?"

"Yes, please and tell her it's very important, it's about Evan."

"About Evan? What's up with Evan?"

"His niece called and said he had a heart attack and he's asking for Saniya."

"Really?!" Jae'mi couldn't believe it either. Suddenly I heard Jae'mi banging on the door through the phone.

"Saniya, Hurry up and get out of the shower!" Jae'mi yelled.

"Dayton, I'll call you right back. I'm going to get Saniya out of the shower."

"Ok Jae'mi... bye."

Click

I hit end call on my phone and waited for Jae'mi or Saniya to call me back. Ten minutes had gone by and Serenity had fallen asleep and she was lying in my arms. I walked into my mom's family room and laid her down in her portable crib. I told my mom I would be back and what was going on with Saniya and Evan. She gave me that concerned look. I smiled and gave her a big kiss on the forehead. I got into my truck and headed out.

I got to Saniya and Jae'mi's house and pulled into the driveway. I walked up to the front door and rang the doorbell. Jae'mi opened the door and I stepped in and saw Saniya. She was sitting on the couch crying. "Saniya, what's wrong?"

"I can't take anymore Dayton. I can't take any more stress; I'm at my breaking point."

"I understand that sweetie, but right now Evan is asking for you, the least you can do is call that young lady back." I couldn't believe those words fell out of my mouth.

"You're right Dayton. May I use your phone please?" I haven't been able to find mine."

"Sure." I handed the phone to Saniya and sat right there next to her on the couch. She found Evan's number and called his niece Heaven back.

"Hello." Saniya said into the phone.

I sat on the couch next to Saniya and held her hand just in case this news was really bad.

I wasn't going to leave Saniya's side before I found out exactly what was going on with Evan.

.

The Sum of My Mistakes

Chapter Thirty-Six

Saniya

After I finished crying and got myself together, I used Dayton's phone to call Evan's niece back. Dayton and Jae'mi both sat on the couch next to me while I dialed the number. Dayton rubbed my hand while I waited for Heaven to answer the phone. "Hello." Heaven said when she answered the phone.

"Hi Heaven, this is Saniya, Evan's friend." I said nervously.

"Hello Saniya! Hello, how are you?" Heaven asked like she knew me already.

"I'm ok, how arc you?" I said feeling quite awkward about this conversation. I had no idea what Evan had told them, and at the same time I didn't want to offend Dayton by acting like I was still Evan's girl.

"Honestly, I'm stressing a lot." Heaven confessed.

"I can imagine." I said feeling a little more relaxed with Heaven. "So how's your uncle doing?" I asked to get to her reason for calling me.

"He's better, thanks for asking." She quickly replied.

I then asked Heaven what happened and she told me he was talking to the kids on the phone and the next thing she knew he was breathing crazy and he began to sweat profusely. Next thing she knew, the doctors were performing CPR on him, shocking his heart and hooking him up to a bunch of machines.

"He's not doing too good Saniya, and he keeps asking for you. Is there any way you can come to North Carolina to see him?" Heaven asked me bluntly.

"Oh Heaven, I'm not sure I can do that, I've been through some things in the past few days and I know my doctors won't clear me to travel quite yet." I lied. I looked over at Dayton and saw the approval on his face. I knew Dayton wouldn't want me to go to NC and I wasn't going to even make it an issue.

"Ok, I understand. Heaven said. She sounded so disappointed.

"Saniya, I know you don't know me and I don't know you, but I'm so scared right now. My father just had a kidney transplant and he's still not out of the woods. I just met Uncle Evan a few days ago and now after donating a kidney to my dad he has a heart attack and I'm here all by myself and I can't take all of this!" Heaven cried into the phone. I was stunned by her reaction to my refusing to come to NC.

"Heaven, please don't cry." I said to her. I'll see what arrangements I can make to get there and I'll call you back." I didn't even look at Dayton to see what his reaction was to my decision to go. I just said my goodbye's to Heaven and hung up the phone.

As soon as I hung up the phone Jae'mi said "You're going to North Carolina to see Evan?" Oh HELL no!" I tried to defend my decision but Jae'mi was just not having it. Then I got the shock of my life.

Dayton looked up at me and said: "You should go Saniya."

"What?" Jae'mi and I said at the same time.

"Yes, I think you should go to see about Evan." Dayton repeated. Jae'mi looked at him like he was crazy. Although I was shocked he said that, I played it off and walked over to the computer and started looking for flights. Jae'mi still stood there in awe and Dayton joined me at the computer.

He put his arm around me and gave my belly a little squeeze. I leaned into his arms and continued to look up flight information for my trip to NC.

"I went to put in the information so I could check the flights to NC. I went to enter 1 passenger and Dayton moved my hand out of the way and clicked on 2 passengers. I looked around at him and he simply said "I'm going with you."

"Ok." I replied.

We boarded the plane the next morning and we landed in NC in the following afternoon. We stopped by the hotel room to check in then headed to the hospital. I walked into Evan's hospital room and saw him lying there. He looked so sick. I was shocked how bad he looked lying in his hospital bed with iv's and all type of machines hooked up to his body. I walked in and said hello to the tired looking yet beautiful young lady with Evan's features, who I assumed was Heaven.

"Saniya?" the young lady hugged me as she asked me my name.

"Yes, I am Saniya, you must be Heaven? I asked just making sure it was her. "Yes, it's me." Heaven responded

"Heaven, this is Dayton Long, the gentleman that made the trip with me."

"Hi Dayton." Heaven said smiling hard at him.

We all traded pleasantries and I took a seat next to Evan's bed. "Evan, its Saniya can you hear me?" I whispered to him. I received no response. I wanted to touch his hand but I didn't want to upset Dayton. I just sat there like a bump on a log. Dayton came and stood behind me and said hello to Evan. He then told me he was going to grab himself some coffee and something quick to eat and he'd be back in a few minutes. He also said I needed some time alone with Evan which shocked me. He kissed me on the cheek and left the room. "Saniya, do you mind if I run out for a few minutes, I want to go check up on my dad." Heaven asked.

"Oh of course you can, I'll be here."

"Thank you, Saniya."

"You're welcome Heaven, take your time."

"Thank you so much Saniya, I haven't been able to catch a break."

"I can imagine."

"He's really been asking for you a lot Saniya, I don't know what the nature of your relationship is, but other than the kids, you're the only one he has been asking for. He keeps telling me he needs to tell you something."

"Really?"

"Yes."

"Thanks Heaven."

"Anytime."

With that Heaven walked out of the door leaving Evan and I alone. I walked back over to the chair next to the bed and sat down. My nausea started and I knew I would throw up at any minute. I rushed into the bathroom and closed the door. I didn't want anyone to hear me throwing up. After I felt better I got myself together, brushed my teeth and went to go sit back down next to Evan. I sat down and took Evan's hand. He squeezed my hand and opened his eyes. "Saniya." he whispered.

"Yes Evan, I'm here." I answered him.

"Saniya, I don't think I'm going to make it out of here."

"Evan, don't say that!" You're going to be just fine; you just need to get some rest."

"Saniya, I need to talk to you."

"I'm right here Evan, talk."

"I need to tell you I'm so sorry about everything."

I sat quietly and listened to Evan.

"I just want to tell you that everything is my fault. Everything you're going through now is because of me."

"Evan, it's not all your fault, I made some stupid decisions, I wasn't thinking straight and I tried to escape the pain I was feeling by going out with Sebastian."

"But if I never cheated you wouldn't have even thought about him."

"All of that is in the past now Evan."

"Not everything Saniya."

"What do you mean Evan?"

"I need you Saniya." I don't want to live without you."

"Evan, can't we talk about this some other time please."

"Ok Saniya, well I wanted to ask you something very serious."

"Sure Evan, what is it?"

"I left everything in my will to you and Azera and Isis and Evan. If I don't make it out of here promise me that you'll see to it that Isis and Evan are taken care of please. If I do make it out of here, I want to marry you Saniya." I want to be with you for the rest of my life."

"Evan, that's a huge responsibility." I said thinking about this baby I was carrying. "

I was in between a rock and a hard place. If I tell Evan yes I know I lose Dayton. If I say no and Evan doesn't make it, what will happen to Evan and Isis? What about this baby? What in the world am I going to do? At that exact moment Dayton walked back into the room. "Everything ok Saniya?"

"Yeah, everything's ok." I lied.

"Really Saniya?" Dayton said not sounding like he was very convinced.

"Yeah Dayton, really." I lied again.

"Well you haven't given him an answer yet Saniya, do you accept his proposal?

The Sum of My Mistakes

Chapter Thirty-Seven

Dayton

When I walked back to Evan's room, I heard him talking to Saniya. I stood

outside the door for a few minutes and listened to their conversation. I

heard Evan ask Saniya to marry him. My heart sank, like the time when

she was in the hospital and he came in and put his arms around her. I knew

I shouldn't break up their little tender moment, but I'm not losing Saniya to

Evan. I will do whatever it is I have to make sure she doesn't stay with

him. Even if that includes taking care of Evan's kids for a while. I care

about her too much to see her with a brother like him. Nothing about Evan

looked like he wasn't going to make it out of this hospital. I knew that was

a sympathy ploy to get Saniya to say yes.

I walked back into the room right as Saniya was stuttering over her words.

I asked her was everything ok wondering if she would tell me what was happening between her and Evan at that moment. I wanted to see how much she trusted me, how much she would tell me. I asked her again was everything ok and she told me yes. She actually lied to me.   Immediately I knew where her loyalties lied and it wasn't with me. I decided to press her even further "Well you haven't given him an answer yet Saniya, do you accept his proposal?" I asked as I stared into Saniya's eyes. She completely froze. I hated putting her under that type of pressure; I just needed to know what she was thinking. "Saniya, say something." I said to her. Still nothing. That was all I needed to know. "I'll take a cab back to the hotel and I'm headed back to NJ Saniya. You apparently have some unfinished business to handle here." I kissed her on the cheek and headed to the hospital exit.

"Dayton!" I heard her yelling behind me. I wanted so badly to just stop and wait for her to come with me, but I just couldn't. I had to get the hell out of there. I had to get out of Saniya and Evan's space. Had to let her make this decision for herself. This was one time where I wouldn't be able to save Saniya. No matter how badly I wanted to.

The Sum of My Mistakes

Chapter Thirty-Eight

Saniya

I called Dayton's name, but he just kept on walking. I didn't know what else to say to him. I was in a bad situation. Evan had just asked me to marry him, I'm carrying his baby and he doesn't even know it. Then there's Isis and Evan. They need someone to be there for them until Asia's better if she ever gets better. I just don't know what to do anymore. I walked slowly back to Evan's room. As I reached the door Heaven came around the corner and saw how upset I was. I was on the verge of a nervous breakdown and you could see it all over my face. "Saniya are you ok?" Heaven asked.

"No." was all I could say to Heaven.

Heaven walked into the room and closed the door.

"Saniya, what's wrong?"

"Your uncle just proposed to me in a weird way. My friend heard it got upset and stormed out and left me."

"Really?" Heaven said not sounding too shocked.

"Heaven, may I use your phone please?" I asked.

"Of course." Heaven said handing me her phone.

I dialed Dayton's number and he sent me to voicemail. I left him a voice message asking him to please call me back as soon as he got the voicemail. I walked back into Evan's room and handed Heaven her phone back. "Saniya." Evan called me from his bed. I had almost forgotten that Evan was laying there. "Saniya, are you ok?" Evan asked.

"Yes Evan, I'm ok." I lied. It seemed to be my MO for the day.

"Saniya, please sit down." Evan asked me, so I again took my seat next to Evan's bed. "So Saniya, what's your answer to my question?"

"Evan, I have no answer for you right now."

"Why not Saniya? It's a simple thing; I promise you I will never betray your love for me. I promise I will never take you through the things that I've been taking you through these past few months. I didn't know how to tell you, but my father came back into my life asking me for a kidney for my brother three months ago. You know what type of relationship I have with my father and I was going through a lot of different emotions. A lot of feelings I couldn't deal with before came out and I wasn't able to handle it. I went off a little and acted an ass. I'm sorry Saniya, I've never been so sorry about anything in my life."

I was shocked at Evan's confession to me. I was very relieved to know what was going on with him. I was also relieved to know my behavior didn't have anything to do with Evan's actions. For once in my life, it wasn't me. After Evan's confession, I knew what I had to do. I got up from my seat and kissed Evan on his forehead. I told him I would be back in a few. I thanked Heaven for calling me and left the hospital. I knew I had to catch up to Dayton. I had to talk to him before he boarded that plane.

I got to the hotel and literally ran to our room. Dayton was packing his things to leave. I was so glad I caught him in time. "Dayton, please don't leave." I begged him.

"Saniya, I can't do this." he said. It looked like he had been crying.

"But Dayton, I didn't do anything." I tried to reason.

"Saniya, what do you want from me?" he asked. "Look how much stuff has happened since we met. It's been constant drama. I can't take anymore. It's too overwhelming and now when it's all said and done, Evan asks you to marry him."

"Dayton, you're acting like I asked him to marry me!" I snapped. I was beginning to get even more upset. Dayton was acting like I had done something to him.

"Saniya, you're carrying the man's child. How can I compete with that?" Dayton was right. What in the hell was I thinking? Once Evan found out about me being pregnant he would never leave me alone. What was I going to do?

"Dayton, please don't leave me, I need you. I know everything is crazy right now, but I really care about you and I want to be with you, if you'll have me. Well if you'll have us." I said as I rubbed my stomach.

"Saniya, are you absolutely sure? You know this is going to get worse before it gets better." Dayton said. His face softened a little and he stopped packing his things and opened his arms for me to hug him.

"I know Dayton, but I think we can get through it together."

"Ok Saniya." Dayton said as he bent down and kissed me on my lips. I was so relieved and so happy to be in Dayton's arms. Then it hit me, What in the world am I going to say to Evan

I kissed Dayton's lips so passionately I got a little dizzy. I stood there in his arms for a while before I looked into his eyes and kissed him again. I just wanted to stay there wrapped in Dayton's arms, but I had to handle one more thing. I had to stand my ground and tell Evan what my decision was. Dayton wanted to come back to the hospital with me, but this was something I had to do by myself. I gave Dayton one more kiss and then I got my stuff together to go back to the hospital.

I got back into our rental car and headed back to the hospital. I found a parking space and walked back into the main doors of the hospital. I got on the elevators back to Evan's floor and was walking down the hallway back to Evan's room when I saw Heaven in the hallway in front of Evan's room door. She was crying hysterically and there were people running in and out of the door. "Heaven, what's wrong?" I asked her. She just kept crying. Finally she got herself together enough to tell me that Evan had had another heart attack. I opened the room door and saw doctors and nurses all over the place working on Evan. They were performing cpr on him and shocking his heart. One of the staff members backed me out of the door and closed it right in front of my face. I hugged Heaven and sat on the floor shocked at what I was seeing. "Oh my God no!"

The Sum of My Mistakes

About The Author

Dawn L Forte' is a native of Plainfield, New Jersey. The mother of two sons and two daughters aged twenty to twenty six. She's also the grandmother of a beautiful three year old granddaughter and adorable two year old grandson. She is a poet in her own right having performed at various open mic nights in the past. This is her first fictional novel. She is currently working on her Second novel and a poetry book.

A victim of Fibromyalgia, A chronic pain disorder Dawn can be found most days at her local Cafe' writing or she can be found relaxing comfortably at home with her grandkids, reading a good book or on her computer writing her second novel. Dawn can be contacted by email at Msd4tae@yahoo.com or Dawn.Forte@gmail.com

CPSIA information can be obtained at www.ICGtesting.com
Printed in the USA
BVOW071246190312

285517BV00001B/6/P